# DOUBLE CROSS COUNTRY

# DOUBLE CROSS COUNTRY

## Joan Murphy Pride

For Gerry—
Enjoy the Trail!
Joan Murphy Pride

## NORTH STAR PRESS OF ST. CLOUD, INC.
### Saint Cloud, Minnesota

First Edition, June 2011

Printed in the United States of America

Published by
North Star Press of St. Cloud, Inc.
P.O. Box 451
St. Cloud, Minnesota 56302

www.northstarpress.com

For my grandchildren

Bennett Murphy Anderson

Carter Douglas Anderson

With love from Nonna

# CHAPTER ONE

I CERTAINLY HADN'T WANTED TO DIE in Wisconsin. It's very cold in Wisconsin in the winter. It seemed even more bone chilling because I was surrounded by six-thousand truly crazy people on cross-country skis. And one of those six-thousand people had just tried to kill me by plunging a sharp, pointed ski pole into the back of my ski jacket. The others were competing in that famous, annual cross-country ski madness in Hayward, Wisconsin, called the Birkebeiner. I was just competing for my life, a commodity of which I am inordinately fond.

"Don't cry, Amy," I kept telling myself. "If you cry, the tears will freeze on your face, your nose will run, and you will be even more miserable and cold than you are right now. Focus on why someone wants to kill you and how to avoid letting that happen."

Outrunning my would-be murderer was out of the question. I never had been able to ski even adequately. The only reason I even had these skinny devil skis on my feet was to please my bosses at Pylon & Voss, the advertising agency where I was a woefully underpaid copywriter, and our big client, Geno Pirelli of Pirelli's Perfect Pasta.

Oh, God, where were all these people now? I'd accused my friends of playing Hansel and Gretel with me. They led me deep into the woods, skied faster than I could, and then left me out there. Until today, I could count on one of them doubling back to see what was holding me up, or, as I darkly suspected, to see what I had broken. But they wouldn't be back today. They were all racing their little hearts out, miles away from me somewhere along the fifty-five-kilometer Birkebeiner trail.

I couldn't count on any help from them until it was too late. The tears came after all, and I'd been right. I was even colder and more miserable than I had been before.

I was angry too because it was ludicrously unfair. How did I get into this mess? As I recalled, it was a deadly series of really bad decisions on my part. I was out on that bumpy fire road, in two-below-zero cold and deep snow to do a favor for our executive art director, Mary Dee Frank, a woman I couldn't stand. She was a world-class bully, a monster boss to the two talented people who worked for her, my friends Peter Andrews and Angela Krajak.

Unlucky me. I had decided to get up early and watch the beginning of the race.

And there was old Mary Dee breathing fire. She screamed that she didn't have the bib with the entry number she needed to wear during the race. She saw me and said, "Find my people and tell them to find my bib and get it to me now."

"Save your breath. I don't work for you," I said, "and I haven't the smallest urge to do you any favors."

She pushed her angry face nearly into mine and snarled, "If I don't have that damn bib on when I cross the checkpoint, I'll be thrown out of the race. And if I am, your little pals will be out of jobs. I told them one of them had to stand by at the start of the race to help me. They aren't here. So they'll have to catch up with me. I'll look for them just before we reach the halfway checkpoint. They better be there and they better have my bib."

With that, she took off her big outer jacket, threw it at me and pushed off to join her wave of skiers starting the race. Mary Dee was selfish enough to ruin my friends' careers over something this small. I was sure of that. I put her jacket on over mine and headed off to look for Angela.

When I put my hands into Mary Dee's big jacket pockets

to stay warm, I felt something. I pulled out a big piece of fabric, which turned out to be the stupid bib. I was sunk. I'd never find Angela in time. I decided I had to try and get the bib to Mary Dee myself. One of the lousiest skiers in the Upper Midwest was about to get into the biggest cross-country ski race in America. Bad decision. If my ski instructor were there, he'd say my being on skis was a little like Madonna singing at High Mass in a nunnery. But I knew I'd have to ski to save my friends' jobs.

I looked around for help and spotted a race helper. I asked him if there was any way I could get the bib to a contestant before she came to the first judges at Seeley, about halfway through the race.

"Can you ski?" he asked, looking at my wonderful new cross-country outfit with what I thought was a definite curling of his lip.

"Can I ski? Can Justin Timberlake sing? Oprah talk? Just tell me where to go to get on the trail."

To pay me back, he did tell me. If I would go down the highway about ten miles, I'd find the Timber Fire Road. It would have fresh snow on it and so, according to him, I could easily ski about a mile in, where I would find the road crossing paths with the Birkebeiner Trail at one of the ten First Aid Stations along the thirty-five mile race.

The starter went on to say, "If your friend left at 8:55 this morning, she should be passing Aid Station Number Three after you arrive. That's at nine kilometers. This is just my best guess, you know, but I think you should have a chance of finding her. If you miss her there you could ski on to the Fire Tower Aid Station."

I laughed to myself, thinking how silly it was that my helpful new friend thought I would ski on. Not a chance. All I planned to do was wait for Mary Dee at Number Three, pass her the numbered bib, if possible, and ski right back down the road. Nothing more. I grabbed the bib and headed for my car.

It was typical of me, I'm afraid, to get thoroughly involved in something truly none of my business and a royal pain in the rear to boot. I drove to the fire road, parked, put on my skis and started out. I knew I didn't ski fast enough and would soon freeze if I wore just my lightweight, but adorable, new cross-country suit. So I zipped up Mary Dee's heavy jacket for warmth and then put her numbered bib over that so that no one would even question my right to be in the vicinity of the race.

I soon found skiing the deserted road to be more of a challenge than I needed or wanted. The next time someone asked me if I could cross country ski, I promised myself that I wouldn't let vanity get in the way and just tell the truth.

"Ski? Of course I don't ski. Do I look like a person who enjoys being cold, miserable and tired? I'm Irish for god's sake. We're an indoor, talky kind of people."

Just when I thought the fire road trail couldn't get worse, it did. I came to the most enormous hill I'd ever seen and no matter where I looked, I couldn't see a way to go around. I'd have to ski right straight down it. As I stood on the lip of the hill, I debated about either taking off my skis and walking down the hill or turning right around and going back out the road to my car. I decided I had to try the hill. As I bent over to take off my skis, I heard a noise, a swish of something coming very close to me. It just bumped me but would have hit me hard if I hadn't bent over right at that moment.

The bump scared me, and I did what I do best on skis. I fell hard and slid down the damn hill. As I bounced and slithered down, I caught a glimpse of something huge and white going by me, like a giant rabbit, a person-sized rabbit on skis. The person

4

didn't have a face, just one of those all-covering ski masks. I also saw something in the snow, as I tumbled by.

Two fresh ski tracks.

When I got to the foot of the hill, by some miracle, I still had both skis and both poles. I struggled to stand up and looked back up the hill. It must have been my imagination. Big white rabbits don't come swooping out of the woods and swipe at you with their ski poles. The snow falling around my feet was just my imagination too. It couldn't be snowing, not with all that blue sky.

I looked closer. What were falling were feathers. Goose down feathers. I looked down at Mary Dee's jacket and it was then that I started to shake with fear. The jacket was ripped from right under my arm straight down to the bottom. Very neatly ripped as though it had been done with an extremely sharp razor or the tip of a very sharp ski pole.

There is nothing like terror to send one flying down a ski trail. It lends wings to the heels of even the most reluctant skier. And so I flew. And pondered on the who, the why and the why me? Whoever had attempted to carve my thumping heart from my chest hadn't really wanted to do it, not to me, not really. The person trying to spear me must have thought I was Mary Dee because I was wearing her jacket, her bib and number, a hat that completely covered my hair and great goggles that were just about bigger than my face. There was a difference in height between Mary Dee and me, but someone in a hurry might not notice that. And someone taking a stab at a person with a ski pole would be bound to be in somewhat of a hurry.

It didn't make me feel any better to know it probably wasn't really me the bunny had been after. I mean, not only had I almost been run through like an olive but also I'd almost died wearing an alias, as it were—and those damn skis to boot.

Life. It was so unfair. So funny. So—a shot of adrenaline—ephemeral.

I sped on, panic being more help than technique, and blessedly soon I saw the long, steady line of skiers crossing the Birkebeiner Trail ahead. I'd come to the juncture and to a rest stop. Now what to do? Should I look for the workers who would be running the rest stop and ask for help? Show them my jacket and make them believe me? It probably would sound like the ravings of a crazy lady.

Anyway, there might not be anyone there who could help. Groups from towns around the race—Cable, Seeley, and Hayward, staffed the rest stops. They were volunteers from groups like Ladies' Aid, Boy Scouts, or Citizen Firemen. Unless there was a lawman there with a walkie-talkie, I couldn't count on any help.

I tried to imagine explaining the situation to the people at the aid station. It sounded like a bad dream, too bizarre to be true. I didn't believe it myself and I was living it. I just couldn't think of anyone who'd want to kill me.

Maybe, and this was a chilling thought, it could have been a random attack by one of those sex fiends one reads about. But I couldn't seriously believe even the most desperate and evil of sexual predators would try anything in four feet of snow in sub-zero cold.

It seemed more logical that the would-be killer was after Mary Dee, who was really a nasty piece of goods and a whole lot more disliked than I was. But disliked enough to kill her? Mess her up a little, sure. But murder?

None of my co-workers seemed to be more than somewhat neurotic. They weren't killer types. Maybe it was just an accident. The skier in white had simply lost his or her balance, put out a ski pole to stop his fall and hit my jacket instead. Then the poor soul had fled, too embarrassed to face me and my feathery fury.

Whatever the truth, I had to make a decision. If I was wrong and there really was a crazed killer stalking me, it'd be suicidal to try returning to my car down that lonely fire road.

It seemed to me that there was only one thing to do and that was to ski on. I could join the seemingly endless line of skiers ski-skating or slip-sliding towards Hayward and a medal. I could leave the trail at Seeley, the twenty-seven kilometers halfway point, and get a ride to Hayward.

I'd pass at least one more rest stop before Seeley. Maybe I could get Mary Dee's bib back to her there. But if I couldn't, I wasn't going to worry. She'd just be disqualified, which was a lot better than my being dead.

# CHAPTER TWO

I SKIED OVER TO THE LINE, waited for a break in the line of skiers going by and then pushed off, just in front of a woman in a purple stretch suit and a hat that proclaimed her to be the best damn skier in Fridley. She gave me a grunting non-welcome and a suspicious look. I could hear her breathing, so close to me it was putting little freeze burns on the back of my neck. Her breathing alternated with little gasps of what sounded like fury. I had gotten ahead of her, but obviously wasn't going fast enough to suit her, and her moans and grunts let me know that she thought I might be adding as least ten seconds to her final race time.

I didn't care. I wasn't going to let Purple Stretch Suit bother me. I was feeling plenty pleased with myself. I hadn't fallen down once so far into my little part of the race — well, not since that hill, but that wasn't my fault, nor was it actually *in* the race yet — and it seemed as though I had made the right choice when I decided to go on.

As a matter off fact, I had half convinced myself that things were going gorgeously. I was slipping and sliding along in wonderful form for me, and I was moving steadily forward.

Then we came to the grandma of all hills. A thick forest of huge trees lined both sides of the sets of tracks. Looking down from the top of the hill, it seemed like I was going over the edge of nothing. Curves and bumps all the way to the bottom. Broken poles and cast-off ski tips dotted the hill. This was the infamous hill before getting to Aid Station Number Five, eighteen and a half kilometers into the race. My friends had spoken of it with awe. It was higher than the Seeley Fire Tower we had just passed.

I couldn't go back. So I closed my eyes and pushed off. I assumed my normal hill position, which was so low to the ground that I could sit down without effort. I had my legs in a snowplow stance powerful enough to clear an airport runway. Even so, I fell three times before I reached the bottom. I took Purple Stretch Suit down with me on my first fall. She was so close to the ends of my skis that when I fell, so did she in a heap of snarling fury. She was still looking for her poles when I went on, slithering and sliding to the foot of the hill. Taking a breath, I looked up. And up and up and up. The hill I had just fallen down now went straight up out of sight and was so steep I could touch the surface of it with my hands by just leaning over a little.

I picked myself up and took off again. I hadn't gone fifty feet before I felt hot breath on my neck. Purple Stretch Suit was right behind me.

"Track," she yelled, "Track!"

I hated doing it but I knew I had to get out of her way and as fast as I could. A good skier would simply have gracefully stepped laterally over to the next set of tracks and let Purple Stretch Suit go whizzing by. Naturally when I tried to step sideways out of the way, I fell. It was a really smashing fall. I fell sort of sideways and sort of frontways going up the next slope. I fell so hard I could hear my knees snap like kindling. *Crack, crack.* They made a lot of noise. They made so much noise that skiers up ahead of me on the hill turned back to look. And then they screamed and screamed. It seemed like everyone on the hill was screaming. I rolled over, sat up and looked to my left. It was Purple Stretch Suit. She was lying down in the snow, like a kid making angels.

What a funny thing to do in the middle of a race, I thought. She was sliding back down the hill, and everywhere she slid, the snow was turning red. An angel in red snow.

I bumped my way over until I was level with her. Her mouth and eyes were open, and she looked surprised. I bent over her and I could see that she wasn't really looking at anything anymore. The best damn skier in Fridley was dead.

I rolled away from her, dizzy and faint and was awfully sick all over the snow. I could feel the cold sweat of fear running down my back, under my arms, down under my ski hat. It was frightening enough seeing violent death so close, so awful. My fear doubled with the thought that it was supposed to have been me lying there making the snow red.

If I hadn't switched tracks, I'd be dead. I was the target. I was the one being hunted through the cold and crowds of the Birkebeiner. It couldn't be a mistake or a random killer. Not after two tries. I had to believe it was a deliberate attempt to kill either me or Mary Dee, the person the killer might have thought I was. My mind insisted on what my emotions had refused to believe until this very moment.

I was being hunted by someone I knew.

# CHAPTER THREE

WITH A LITTLE HELP FROM A MURDERER, I had managed to bring the giant Birkebeiner to a screaming, sobbing, complete halt. Skiers were piled up in a solid mass on the lip of the hill behind us. The up-hill ahead was full of skiers who had stopped, turned around to see what was wrong and were frozen in place by shock or curiosity. And down at the bottom of the hill, besides the dead Fridley woman and me, were dozens of skiers who had crashed into each other and piled up trying to avoid the body.

The race officials were frantic. One of them slid down to me and soon joined me in throwing up at the sight of the body. Then he pulled out his cell phone and called for help. A loud-speaker announcement told all the skiers to stay right where they were, that the sheriff was on his way. They stopped the clock for all the skiers from our position back to the final wave. The Birkebeiner was shut down cold.

The race starts in Cable in Bayfield County and ends at Hayward in Sawyer County. They decided to call both sher-iffs. On race day, both would be somewhere on the trail. While we waited, I was shaking with fear and cold and wishing, wishing that my One True Thing was here with me. That's what I call my longtime honey and someday husband, Ryan Kelly. I loved him but we'd had a little bad session after a party where I'd flirted wildly, and he hadn't called me since. He wasn't here today because I hadn't invited him, to get even. I closed my eyes and pretended Ryan was with me. When I opened them my fear was almost gone. I was sad and angry instead. I looked at poor Purple Stretch Suit, and my anger turned to fury. The murderer had put a little backbone into me. How dare anyone take another person's life? I felt guilty too because I was still alive and the body next to me was supposed to be mine. This was personal. I wanted to avenge both of us and try and find out who had murdered her.

The sheriff of Bayfield County was first to arrive. He was Joe Bear, an Ojibwa from the Red Lake Reservation and a very famous man in Northern Wisconsin. He arrived on a winter-equipped ATV, wearing jeans, boots, a wool shirt and a great cowboy hat complete with feathers.

He also arrived gorgeous. Tall, bronzed, muscular and slim hipped. He had such dark-brown eyes they were almost black and the whitest teeth in Wisconsin. I mean, I was still in shock and plenty worried and nervous, but some things a gal can't help but notice, right?

Deputies started arriving from every direction. This wasn't surprising. On the day of the race, most of the deputies of both counties were close. Officials had already sent paramedics to the scene and called the Bayfield County Coroner who was manning one of the aid stations a few miles down the trail. The sheriff of Sawyer County, Sam Nelson, was next. He was a spit-and-polish man in an immaculate uniform.

Both sheriffs listened to my story of why I thought I should have been the victim and why the bullet had struck poor Purple Stretch Suit instead. I was still sitting in the snow because, hard as I tried, I couldn't get up. My skis were still on my feet, in line with the body, and it was obvious that if I hadn't fallen, I would have been the one shot.

After telling me to stay put, Joe and Sam got together to get jobs divided between them. Joe had gotten the case so he was in charge. Anyone could see that the almighty mess of the race situation made it important for them to work together and quickly.

Joe made an announcement on a portable loud speaker to the crowd. "Stay exactly where you are. Do not move. We don't want this scene to be any more messed up than it already is. We'll get you going as soon as possible."

"The first thing to do," Sam said, "is to get rid of as many skiers as we can. We'll send them home."

Joe asked, "How you going to do that, Sam?"

"Well, I'm not a skier, so I don't know the trail but I think we're close to Cable."

"There are about four-thousand skiers waiting to come down that hill. So the trail behind the skiers is blocked all the way back to Cable."

Sam thought a second and then said, "Well, we better get buses."

"There aren't enough buses in Northern Wisconsin to get them all out of here. Anyway, a bus can't get in here on that Timber Fire Road. Too narrow, too hilly. Impossible."

"So what can we do with them?" asked Sam.

"We're going to get them out of the woods the same way they got in. On skis. We'll get the vital crime scene work here done as fast as we can. We'll check all the skiers for weapons. Then the ones who could not be involved will ski out. The officials can start the clock again and the race will continue."

"God, Joe, that'll take hours," Sam said with a worried frown.

"It had better not." Joe said seriously. "We have to get them going in forty minutes or less. Otherwise it'll get too dark to get the slower ones all the way out.

"If you think we've got problems now, imagine hundreds of skiers on these big hills in the dark. So let's go. The deputies can check all the skiers for weapons, get their names and bib numbers. The folks here at the bottom of the hill and close to the scene, should be detained. We won't let any of them leave. There are about two dozen, I'd guess. Ask them to take off their skis and wait by the judges' desk. We will have to get them out. They're our most likely witnesses."

"I'll get my guys to do that," Sam said. "What will your crew be doing?"

"We'll do all the very preliminary crime-scene work we can," Joe said. "Most of it will have wait for the State Crime Lab to arrive. We'll secure the area and leave the body here until they get here. After they're done, they can send the body for autopsy."

Within minutes, Joe had cordoned off the area around the body and me by sticking broken ski poles in the snow around us and wrapped yellow crime tape around the poles. I was still sitting right next to the body. I had been told not to move until they photographed the body from every direction.

I was in on everything, which pleased me, kind of. But Joe Bear turned out to be not so much fun. The only thing he'd said to me over and over was a crabby, "Don't move your legs. As a matter of fact, don't move anything at all until I say you can." Later he added, "I don't want to lose any clues that you might damage thrashing around. So stay perfectly still. When we're done here, I'll take you out myself. Until then, don't even think about going anywhere."

I was too shaky to move anyway so I didn't argue with the gorgeous but chauvinistic sheriff of Bayfield County, although he needed taking down several pegs. I'd spend my time instead trying to remember why I was at the Birkebeiner at all or why I thought I could or should ski in it. It made my usual buttinski behavior seem like tiny flaws.

It had started one day at the ad agency when Geno Pirelli announced that he was planning a gourmet spaghetti dinner for the big name Birkebeiner skiers from all over the world. It would be good publicity for Pirelli's Perfect Pasta. He wanted agency help planning and promoting it and every member of the creative team to be present for the race and party. That included little, sniveling, rotten skier, me.

I have never understood the beauty of winter sports. I've asked my friends, "Why do you love it so? You come in exhausted with eyes nearly frozen shut and great patches of frostbite on your hands and feet. It's positively masochistic."

"It isn't. It's bred into us. The solitude, the challenge."

"The sheer lunacy," I'd said. "The pain, the sore throat, the pneumonia."

My brain was frying trying to think of a good excuse why I must stay in the Twin Cities. Then Geno added, "Remember, Mama skied in the Olympics for Italy in 1950 and considers the Birkebeiner to be sacred and a command performance."

I didn't even try to argue. Mama Pirelli was feared, loathed and the almost total owner of Pirelli's Pasta. She was the one who made my paycheck cashable. I was going skiing.

And so there I was, cold, scared, and sitting next to a dead body. A crew arrived with a portable screen that they set up all around the marked off area. The medical examiner arrived and began an examination of the body. Joe Bear was busy giving orders to, what was by now, an army of deputies. Plus he took measurements of everything, wrote what looked like a book full of notes and took a zillion pictures.

I was getting dizzy from the flashes. And I was getting madder and madder. That stuck-up sheriff hadn't even bothered asking me if I knew anything. Wasn't worried if I froze to the ground. He was treating me like a suspect. Me, the innocent victim.

Tiny tears of self-pity threatened to spill, but I fought them down with the knowledge that they'd made me look even more ugly than I already did. I had a puffy nose, gummy eyes and worse, the heady aroma of I've-just-been-sick surrounding me. I looked bad and smelled worse. I didn't want to add to the horror.

I couldn't imagine why I cared what the stuck-up sheriff thought. Obviously, I was dealing with an ego the size of the Himalayas, one even bigger than my own. This was a man I could never be interested in beyond a superficial physical attraction. So I just tried to relax and think about who might be the killer. I had more facts than that good-looking sheriff did and I also knew all the people who might be involved. I could just imagine the look of surprise and the abject apologies when he learned that it wasn't really me who had been the intended victim, but Mary Dee. Not to mention his chagrin and the shame he would feel when I handed him the name of the murderer plus all the facts needed to get an airtight conviction.

The coroner called Joe back to the body and told him what he had found in his preliminary examination. Naturally, because I was still sitting by the body, I heard every word. Even in my cold and weakened condition, I was glad to be on the inside so to speak. This would all come in handy when I solved the crime and solved it a damn sight faster than Joe Bear.

"The entrance wound makes it pretty certain, Joe, that the shot was fired from a lot higher up. The entry path indicates that she was shot from somewhere on the east side of the hill. My best guess right now would be from a point in the trees about halfway up the hill. You might look for a deer stand. The wound looks like a rifle shot, a hunting rifle probably. We won't know until the autopsy when we can get a better look at the wound or until you find the shell or the casing, if you can find anything in all this mess."

Joe said, "We'll search, but it'll take time to sift through all this snow."

The coroner agreed with a nod. "Right now, we need to file the time of death and notify her emergency contact. How soon can we get that information?"

Joe said, "It's going to be easy to identify the victim. There's that big number, right on her bib. All her information will be on file with the Birkebeiner office in Hayward. They're really professional, very efficient."

After sending his men slowly up the hill, looking for the spent cartridges or any signs of where the murderer was when he did his shooting, Joe collected what had been found. All the evidence was either carefully packed in small plastic bags and labeled or covered over and numbered for the State Crime Lab.

Joe put his deputy in charge and then motioned for me to get up and carefully leave the enclosed scene of the crime. I didn't move.

Finally he spoke. "C'mon, Miss, we have a race to start, a lot of cold people to get going. You and I will go to my office in Cable where I can take a statement from you."

"I certainly would get up if I could," I said snappishly, "but I find I can't move my legs."

"That's because you're sitting on one of your skis and have the other one on top of it. See? Roll over a little way, and I'll try to get the binding up. Didn't anyone ever teach you how to fall so that you didn't land on top of your skis?"

I certainly didn't reply to that fatuous remark. I simply gave him my best so-cold-it-could-kill look.

Joe continued, "Just leave the skis here. They'll be safe."

"I hope not," I said. "I hope somebody steals the damn things so I never have to put them on again."

"Yes, I can see you've had a bad day. Well, we'll climb the hill and then you can hop on the back of my ATV and hang on. We'll get the race going and then go to my nice, warm office where I can question you while you thaw out."

Joe pushed and pulled me and finally got the two of us back up the hill. Then he gave a signal, and the officials hurried down the hill, marking new lanes and closing off others so as to avoid the crime area and to keep the skiers safe.

They had sorted things out, made the announcement that the race would continue and started the clock again.

The skiers moved down the hill again. It was an awesome sight, the way it always is at the beginning of the race when thousands are grouped in waves together at the starting lines. Luckily, cross-country skiers pride themselves on their sportsmanship, and the lines flowed down the hill in more or less perfect order. *They are good sports*, I thought and felt absurdly proud of all of them. In spite of my well-known antipathy to anyone who thrived in cold or snow, I had to admit cross-country skiers were good sports.

# CHAPTER FOUR

THE TRIP OUT OF THE WOODS ON THE back of Sheriff Joe Bear's ATV was certainly a lot faster than my ski in and a lot more fun too. I had to hang on to Joe very tightly because he drove really fast. Actually, that wasn't as unpleasant as one might think. Joe was very warm and smelled like fresh, cold air with a hint of wood fire. Gradually my shaking stopped, and I started thinking a little more clearly. When we got back down the fire road and out onto the highway, Joe put me into his RV, and then loaded the ATV onto a trailer. He told me he'd send someone back for my car and would give me a ride back from Cable to Telemark when we were done with the questioning if I was too shaken up to drive.

He couldn't take any statements from me until he had a witness and some official way of taping the interview but he did ask me, on the drive to Cable, if I had any idea of what was going on or who might be involved.

"Not quite yet," I said. "I need to talk to some people and then sit down quietly and go over everything I know about them. I should have it figured out in a few days. Of course, proving it will take a little longer."

Joe let out a sound that might have been a snort or a smothered laugh. I was pretty sure he was laughing at me because I could see his shoulders shaking. This is a man, I thought, who needs a little taking down. All modesty aside, I was just the woman to do it. I was going to have to be careful how I went about it though. I didn't want to make him angry or to dislike me so much that he wouldn't let me be part of the investigation.

"I'm glad to see that a little thing like murder hasn't seriously shaken your self-confidence," Joe said. "Most women would be a little scared after someone shot at them."

"Oh," I said, "no one was shooting at me."

"Then the murderer was a damn lousy shot. You heard the preliminary ballistics report. He was aiming right at you. So who do you think the victim was supposed to be?"

"I'm pretty sure they were just shooting at the jacket and bib number. Mary Dee Frank's jacket and bib number. She's one of the people in the group I'm here with at the race. You see, I was wearing her jacket and bib."

Joe gestured to me to stop and quickly got on his cell phone. He asked for his deputy in command at the Birkebeiner and told him to find and detain Mary Dee.

Then he pointed at me to continue.

I said, "I have absolute proof they weren't aiming at me. The fact is I don't really ski and everyone knows that."

"You signed up to ski in one of the greatest world races and you don't ski?" Joe looked at me like I'd lost my mind. "You're an amazing woman."

I certainly had to agree with that, and yet I didn't think he meant it to be quite as complimentary as I would have liked. In fact, it smacked of a certain juvenile sense of humor. Joe soon said something that proved my suspicions.

"So how did you get this Mary Dee's bib and jacket? You haven't—ah—done something to her, have you, Amy?"

"Sarcasm is a sign of a very shallow mind. And I don't recall giving you permission to use my first name."

Whoops. I remembered I wanted to make friends with Joe so that I could get his help in solving the crime, so I quickly said, "Actually, I don't really mind if you call me Amy. Please do."

"And you can call me anything you like, but I prefer Joe. Why do you think Mary Dee was supposed to be the victim? Do people dislike her?"

"Heavens, yes. She's pure poison. But dislike is a long way from murder."

At this point we arrived at Cable and parked in front of the Sheriff's Office. It was a new building of polished logs with great, high glass windows. I thought how perfect it was for these beautiful and wild woods and how it seemed to fit Joe to a tee. It was obviously brand new and yet it looked like it had always belonged in these northern woods. When we got inside, Joe introduced me to Deputy Inga Johnson, a tall, cool blonde who looked me up and down. She didn't look like she was impressed, and she didn't look even a little bit friendly. She had blue-agate eyes and stand-up-and-salute little breasts that looked like they were made of industrial plastic.

Joe gave her some instructions for setting up the interview room and getting the tape ready and then he asked her to make me comfortable and bring me anything I might want. He went off to check with his staff to find out what was going on and if there were any problems.

Deputy Johnson and I walked around each other for a minute after Joe left, like two cats getting ready to pounce. Finally she said, "I can get you some coffee. It's been brewing since this morning so it's plenty strong."

"Thanks but I'd prefer fresh coffee." I said. "I'm sure it won't take you too long to make it, and I really don't feel I'll be able to talk to Joe without it."

Ah, two direct hits. She'd have to make the coffee and she didn't like me calling the sheriff Joe, not one little bit. *Damn, I'm good.*

When Joe got back, he started the tape, announced the date and exact time, said his name and spelled it, then my name, address, age, and marital status—was that really necessary?—and added the name of the witness, Inga Johnson.

"Miss Connelly. Tell me about the people you're with here in Hayward and why you think they might be involved in this crime."

I went back over my reasons—the bib, the jacket—for thinking the victim might or should have been Mary Dee. Then I added that I believed if she were the intended victim, I thought it logical that the murderer would be someone she knew. It must be a person who had come to the Birkebeiner with us. A person we knew well.

"Can you please name these people for me and tell me the relationship?"

"Of course," I said. "There are thirteen in our group. Everyone is involved in some way with Pirelli's Perfect Pasta in Minneapolis. Half of the people work directly for Pirellis or are married to someone who does. The other half are from their advertising agency, Pylon and Voss, and we all work on the Pirelli account or are married to someone who does."

I stopped to get a count and then said, "Those from Pirelli's Perfect Pasta include Geno Pirelli, the CEO of the company and his wife, Lucia Antonucci Pirelli; Mama Pirelli, Geno's mother and the founder and chief stockholder of Pirelli's; her chauffeur, Stephano, whom she brings everywhere with her; Mac Larson, the Pirelli legal counsel; and last, Mac's mother, Harriet Smythe-Larson, who somehow managed to get herself invited on the trip."

I took a breath and went on. "The people in the group from Pylon and Voss include me, Amy Connolly, copywriter; Mary Dee Frank, head of the art department; Peter Andrews, a graphic designer who works for Mary Dee; Angela Krajak, Mary Dee's assistant; Chuck Pylon, agency president and head of Creative; and his wife, Virginia. Our agency CEO and chairman is somewhere up here with his wife but not involved with those of us staying at Telemark."

Joe turned off the tape and said, "That's quite a long list, Amy. I don't think I'll be able to keep track of it without a good chart. Officer Johnson, please copy that list off the tape and get it to me ASAP. Then I'd like you to start background checks on these people."

Joe turned back to me. "In the meantime, I hope, Amy, that you'll help me with descriptions of these people. And with any reasons you can think of why they might wish Ms. Frank harm."

My heart sank. I knew a lot of reasons my co-workers had for disliking Mary Dee. Some of them I wouldn't mind watching as they were being carted off to jail. But ratting on my friends? Too hard. Some of the nicest people I knew had been the most damaged by Mary Dee.

"I just don't want to rat out my friends." I said. "I have to go on working with these people, you know, and if I'm wrong about their reasons for hating Mary Dee, it might ruin their lives."

"Nothing about murder is easy. You have to remember that, if you're right, one of these people is a killer. Killers make very poor friends and co-workers. This person missed killing the woman he or she was after this morning and will almost certainly try again. You could prevent a second murder, and it could be yours. The killer must be wondering how much you saw this morning, what you noticed, what you know."

"I know you're right. I'm a little scared," I said. "Let me think about it. I'll help you if I can, but I want to be sure I'm not pointing a finger at the wrong person. I do know who I wish was guilty — Mary Dee."

"Well, tell me what you know about her. The key to most murders is usually found in the character and personality of the victim. And remember whatever you choose to tell me will be kept strictly between us. No part of it will ever be made public unless it has an immediate connection to the murder."

"I don't mind ratting on Mary Dee," I said. "She's the head of the art department and a bully who uses her title to make everyone who works for her miserable. She's a genius at creative review meetings where she can steal and take credit for more creative ideas in one session than most people could in a lifetime. She's fairly good-looking, completely selfish, and we all think she uses sex to get what she wants. Even slimier, she loves to find out things about people and then makes jokes about them in the most public way she can."

"She sure sounds like a co-worker from hell," Joe said. "But can you be more specific? For example, the sex. Was she involved with someone in the agency or at Pirelli's?"

"Knowing her, probably more than one. You'll have to find that out for yourself. Right now I've said all I think I can. Oh, gosh. I just remembered that I forgot to tell you about the big white bunny."

I told him the whole story, and I couldn't tell if he thought I had slipped a wheel or was just overly imaginative. So I let the bunny drop. But I knew it had to have something to do with our mystery. And some day Joe would be sorry he hadn't taken it more seriously.

He continued to try to dig more information out of me, but I really wanted to think before I spoke, a new experience for me. I wanted to give him the names of some of the more awful of the people in our group, but for the life of me I couldn't imagine what they might have against Mary Dee that was a strong enough motive for murder.

Take Mac Larson's mother, a snob of epic proportions. Wouldn't it be fun to see her scrubbing some prison toilets? And I wouldn't mind the murderer turning out to be that short, fat malevolent matriarch, Mama Pirelli. She ran the business and her family with a heavy Italian thumb. She hated Mary Dee because she thought she was involved with Geno. Mama was clever, suspicious and, I'd heard, extremely dangerous when crossed. She couldn't have done it though. She was too old and out of shape. The thought of her chasing through the woods on skis was hilarious. Of course she could have used spooky Stephano, her chauffeur. He was in good enough shape, and everyone said he did anything Mama told him to do.

Joe finally gave up and said he'd drive me back to my car if I felt well enough to drive. I did but I wanted a little more time with him so I said I was a tad faint.

So he drove me to Telemark instead and said he'd get my car delivered later. On the way, he kept trying to change my mind about fingering my friends, but I wasn't ready to share.

Joe also kept stressing the fact that I might be in danger. He kept up a litany of advice. Do this, don't do that. I just rolled my eyes and said, "Okay, okay."

"No, really listen. This is serious. Do not, I repeat, do not discuss the murder or your ideas of who might have done it with anyone but me."

"I won't."

"Stop rolling your eyes and listen," Joe said. "I'm serious. Be careful. Don't go out alone. Don't go anywhere where there aren't a lot of people. Don't ask questions. Don't even stare at people too long. Don't trust anyone in your group or tell them anything. Keep out of it from now on."

"Okay, I'll be careful and I won't do anything stupid. I'll follow your advice at all times."

"And for God's sake, Amy, don't try to solve this by yourself or tell anyone that you intend to try and solve it. Promise me. "

This was going to be difficult to respond to without lying as I had every intention of starting my interrogations as soon as I got into the hotel. "I won't," I said, carefully crossing my legs as I said it. This is as good as crossing your fingers when you don't intend to keep a promise but a lot less noticeable.

I needed to see Joe again to solve the murder, so I said, "I'm sure I'll be getting more ideas when I calm down, get some rest, so maybe it would be good to have . . . your cell phone number, so I can call you when I do." I gave him puppy eyes, innocence personified.

Actually, I was hoping he'd give me his home phone number. Some information on his current romantic attachments would be helpful too.

Joe shook his head. "No, I do not want you calling me with your new ideas. People are bound to see or hear you. I don't want anyone thinking you're involved with the police. That would be a red flag to anyone who wants to know how much you know or suspect. You must act like you know nothing that is not common knowledge."

I was miffed and let it show. "I think you're going to lose a valuable resource if you won't accept my phone calls. Without that jacket and bib number, how can I be in danger? Anyway I can handle it myself."

"Sorry. You know, this phone is the property of Bayfield County. I'm not allowed to get personal calls from hot, young women on it. I'll give you my cell number but don't call unless it's a crisis."

"I find myself seriously doubting that you get sexy calls on any phone. All you're doing is making bad jokes, ignoring my help and not appreciating what a great clue you've got in that bunny."

Joe laughed and then said, "Amy, I took your bunny tale very seriously. Actually your story about getting slashed on the fire road makes me pretty sure you know the murderer. You probably work with him or her. You're going to have to be very,

very careful around the members of your group. Pretend you know absolutely nothing and didn't see a thing. This includes people you now count as friends. When I want to get in touch with you, I'll have Officer Johnson call and arrange a meeting. You can tell your friends she's an old college friend."

Of course I was disappointed not to be a part of the police activity and positively bilious at having to deal with Joe through the snow queen. But I was encouraged by the fact that Joe seemed worried about me.

He was interested. He was definitely interested. And to my everlasting shame, so was I.

# CHAPTER FIVE

The lobby at Telemark was jammed full of skiers who had finished the race. They were all talking a mile a minute about the murder and telling each other what a great race they'd had and how it'd have been even better except for poor skiers who had gotten ahead on the track and slowed them down. They paid no attention to me, probably couldn't see me because I was short. These women were tall, with legs that started in Minnesota and ended in Iowa. All the skiers were still wearing their skin-tight racing suits, and they all had awesome bodies. Not a lump or a bump anywhere. This was a good reason to stay clear of cross-country people. Well, the women anyway.

An Italian had won the race hours ago. After watching all the skiers leave Telemark, it occurred to me that if I had stopped for a cup of coffee and a bagel, gotten into my car, driven the seventeen miles to Hayward, searched for a place to park, the race might have been won before I finished parking. And the finish of the Birkebeiner was typically as exciting as the start. The skiers came flying into Hayward and went right down Main Street, which had been packed with snow. The sidewalks were full of shouting happy people eager to congratulate the finishers. And they cheered for everyone, from the leaders to the last skiers, the ones who might not be in until sundown.

The TV was on full blast with coverage of the race and of the murder. I had to turn away and felt my eyes filling with tears as I watched a shot of the poor dead skier. She was partially covered but I could see she was still wearing her purple stretch suit, and she was still out there on that hill, cold and dead.

The first friend I saw was Peter Andrews, a really great graphic designer, equally brilliant on the board and the computer. I loved working with him and counted him as one of my very best friends at Pylon and Voss. He waved frantically at me from across the room and started slowly towards me, pushing his way through the crowd.

Peter looked even more disheveled than usual. He was very tall and stick thin. Today he looked almost skeletal in his racing suit. It was hard to know just how tall he was because he hunched even when walking. He had thin, straight, flyaway hair and big, brown, puppy dog eyes behind thick glasses. He was great fun to be with after work. We usually had wine and settled in cozily for a nice, malicious talk about all the baddies and no-talents at the agency and some moron clients.

At work he was so nervous I thought he might someday shake right out of his skin. This was because Mary Dee treated him like a slave even though it was mainly Peter's talent, which she takes total credit for, that kept her job secure.

Finally Peter worked his way to my side. "Oh, Amy, I've been so worried about you. I was frantic when I saw you out in the cold sitting right next to a dead body. They said *you* had been shot at. I thought I'd never see you again."

My jaw dropped. "How in the world did you know I was involved in the murder?"

"Your picture's been all over television for the past three hours."

"You saw me on TV? How could that have happened? I didn't see any TV crews or even a camera out there in the woods or even on the trail."

"Cell phones, Amy. I'll bet every other person in the race had a camera cell phone along. And everyone around you took your picture and a lot of them e-mailed shots right off to WCCO-TV and KSTP-TV. After just a little while, it was on all the stations, even CNN. A murder at the Birkebeiner is news all over the world."

"How did I look?" I asked, imagining talent scouts and modeling agencies frantically trying to get hold of me. Not to mention interviewers from magazines, newspapers and radio and TV stations who surely were all hot to get my exclusive story—Brave Little Ad Writer Nearly Writes THE END To Life.

Peter dashed that swell dream. "Well, actually you didn't look too good. You were throwing up in almost every shot."

*That* moment. Everyone had to capture that moment. Right. I felt like I'd be good and sick all over again. The thought of maybe millions of people watching me puke was bitter, so bitter.

Peter continued to be concerned. "Why was someone trying to kill you Amy? Are you still terrified? "

"No, I'm fine. No one was trying to kill me."

"How do you know? Maybe you did something or know something you shouldn't. Maybe a madman has targeted you. The killers were aiming at you. All the news reports said so. Trajectories . . . something like that."

"No, they weren't. The sheriff doesn't seem to think so. He thinks it was probably just an accident or a hunter with a bad sense of direction."

I felt a little guilty lying to Peter like that. But until I knew who might be involved, I was going to try to keep my dear little rear-end as safe as I could. I needed to change the subject fast.

"Is Mary Dee back in yet? Have you seen her? I saw you talking to her this morning, and you looked like someone had hit you with a shovel. What was that all about?"

"Oh, God, that bitch. That bitch!"

"Peter, for heaven's sake. What's she done to you?"

"That sneaky, nasty, conniving, filthy thief. I could kill her."

I could hardly believe my ears. Sweet, quiet Peter. I didn't think I'd ever heard him so angry before, and Mary Dee had done lots that should have provoked him. This anger was new and frightening.

"Of course she's always been a rotten stinking liar and thief, Peter. But she's not worth killing and going to jail for. What specifically has she done to you now?"

Peter gulped, "She stole my idea on the new line of frozen Pirelli pastas and sauces. The one I've been working on for weeks. It was the best thing I've ever done, and she just took it. She went right to Geno Pirelli with it on Wednesday. Pawned it off as hers. She knew I was going to present my idea on Thursday to the Creative Review Board, and she got to Pirelli first and claimed it as her own. Now who will believe it was mine, Amy?"

"I believe you. And I'll talk to Geno if you want me to. But he's known for having a soft spot for Mary Dee. Why, only God knows. I've always had my suspicions though. She must be doing him some big favors. Maybe she's spying on everyone for him or teaching him new perversions."

"I can't stop thinking of how much I want to see her dead and gone, out of my life for good."

I felt sorry for Peter, but I felt scared too. If he had anything to do with the shooting this morning, he had to have thought he was shooting at Mary Dee. And now I knew how much he hated her. And he knew I knew. God, this was getting complicated.

Suddenly he started to cry. "I was counting on that campaign. I thought it'd give me enough confidence to go to Pylon and ask—no demand—a raise. Mark and I want to buy a house. We've found a perfect little bungalow just a block from Lake Harriet."

Mark Rollings was Peter's partner and opposite. He was short, a little plump, with black, curly hair and he was always laughing and having fun. We all loved him and Peter adored him. I tried to comfort Peter as best I could with promises of open warfare on Mary Dee and support with the agency chiefs. Soon he quit crying but I couldn't get a smile from him. He still looked as if he wanted to murder Mary Dee when we parted.

I hadn't had more than coffee since breakfast, many long hours ago, but first I really needed a shower. I hurried up to my room and cleaned up and then went down to Telemark's big restaurant for a little lunch. Someone called my name from the back of the room. It was Angela Krajak, my roommate at the Birkebeiner.

I could have predicted she'd be sitting in the very last booth with her back right up against the wall. Angela didn't like people looking at her. It was such a damn shame. She used to be one of the most beautiful creatures God put on this earth.

Then she met Mary Dee. At the time, Angela was a model, just starting out and looking for her big break. Mary Dee had hired her for a few shots, and Angela had begun to trust her advice. Big mistake. Huge mistake. Mary Dee was the number one fan of cosmetic surgery. She'd had every part of her body lifted, added to, cut away, or waxed. There's no virgin territory on Mary Dee.

She talked Angela into having her head rounded out with silicone. She convinced Angela that the back of her head was too flat and that she desperately needed this surgery if she wanted to get the Kiss My Kurls Beauty Salons modeling business. It was something the doctors had never tried before but Mary Dee talked them into it.

About a month after the surgery, the entire lump of silicone the doctors had inserted shifted and slid down, most of it ending under the skin on the back and sides of Angela's neck. A bad infection followed and spread to her face. Many operations later, Angela had terrible scars and no hair at all on the back of her head.

Mary Dee was never one to feel remorse. We were amazed to hear that she'd found Angela a new job. Not just a new job, she kept telling us, but a whole new career. Angela's swell new job turned out to be an assistant to Mary Dee and the whole new career was being worked like a slave for peanuts.

I slid into the booth and grabbed a menu. Then I looked up at Angela. She was frowning and looked nervous.

"Angela, what's wrong? You look worried. Mary Dee being her usual rotten self?"

"Well, yes, but that's not it. We can't talk here. Can you come up to the room as soon as you're finished eating? I need to ask you about something. I just can't figure it out, and I've thought and thought about it."

"Can't you give me a hint? You're being very mysterious."

Her eyes shifted around the room. "No, it might not be safe. We can't talk here. Oh, it's probably nothing. I'm really scared because of the murder. But I saw someone not in the right place, shouldn't have been there. Come to our room, Amy, and I'll tell you what I saw."

I promised to eat quickly and head up to our room pronto. I scarfed down my lunch as fast as I could, adding to the problems my ordinarily steel stomach had been subjected to already today. It certainly sloshed around when I thought about my time with the gorgeous Sheriff Bear. I felt so disloyal to Ryan. I loved that guy like crazy and I wanted to marry him in a few more years. He wanted to get more serious now but I thought we'd been having too much fun to start acting old. Plus I thought the fact I couldn't seem to stop flirting with other guys showed I wasn't ready to settle down.

Well, I decided to think about that later and just not worry about my somewhat innocent cheating. Thinking about it made my head hurt. I wanted to put my conscience to rest for a while. Ryan understood me, loved me, knew my flirting wasn't serious, would always forgive me and be there for me. I had to concentrate now on solving the murder and finding out what Angela knew.

I had almost reached the safety of Angela's and my room when a door popped open into the hall and Mrs. Smythe-Larson appeared. Oh, ghastly appearance.

Mrs. Smythe-Larson was not too wonderful looking, at best. She was heavily corseted with iron-gray hair in a don't-you-dare-touch-me rows of curls. She had cement eyes and a narrow, pursed mouth. And today she was angry, which mottled her heavy cheeks and narrowed her eyes and mouth to mere slits. I'd heard she feared that I was after her son, Pirelli's attorney, Mac Larson. Mac did have a thing for me in his blue-blooded, bloodless sort of way. This maddened Mrs. Smythe-Larson, who lived to see Mac become someone big in Conservative and WASP politics. I had assured both mother and son that I wasn't the least bit interested in helping Mac climb that particular ladder, but neither seemed to hear me. Or believe me.

She was breathing hard as she spoke. "Miss Connolly, I've been waiting for you. Step into my rooms, please. I want to have a word with you."

"Mrs. Smythe-Larson, I'm really too tired right now. Perhaps tomorrow."

"Tomorrow might be too late for dear Mac, the way you carry on."

"Excuse me?"

"I hear you caused an ugly scene during the Birkebeiner."

"You mean the murder? I certainly did not cause that."

"I've been told that someone was trying to kill you. I can certainly believe that."

"You're too kind, " I said sarcastically.

"I want you to stop seeing Mac. You are simply not our sort."

"Well, thank God for that."

"Don't be impertinent. And pay attention. You are not to go chasing after my son. You are not to see him outside of business hours at all."

I hadn't even *started* seeing Mac, but all at once, I was so angry at his mother's bossy, prejudiced attitude that I snapped and said, "And why shouldn't I do that?"

"You will ruin his life. You're a hoyden, a troublemaker, and worst of all, you're Catholic. He's running for the state legislature now. Who knows how far he can go? Without you, that is. You could stop his chances of becoming Minnesota's youngest governor."

"He doesn't seem to mind. Actually he hinted to me that he might turn Catholic after his last speech in St. Paul's Hispanic neighborhood."

Mac had never said anything like that, but I knew it would madden his super prejudiced mother.

She turned red. "Don't be ridiculous! That was just politics, which I know you couldn't possibly understand. When he wins his district, he'll find some reason for changing his mind."

"You call lying to the public, politics? I'm glad I don't understand politicians. But Mac should fit right in our legislature."

"Only if he has a chance. And he won't have that chance if he associates with you. Promise me that you'll leave him alone."

Fighting nausea at the thought of being a permanent part of Mac's life, I fixed Mrs. Smythe-Larson with a glare and said, "I don't think I can do that. I find him too—ah—interesting."

Her hue darkened, and her eyes went to slits. "There are ways of making you stop. I hear your sister-in-law would like to join the Junior League. And how much do you like your job? I don't suppose you know that I'm a big stockholder of Pirellis."

"Short of murdering me, Mrs. Smythe-Larson, I can't think of any possible way of your making me do anything I don't feel like doing."

"Well, accidents do happen."

# Chapter Six

It was either slap Mrs. Smythe-Larson until she passed out or leave the scene. I couldn't trust myself to talk to her because the only words I could think of at the moment were rather crude. So I simply gave her a very lady-like salute with a finger, turned on my heel and departed. The sound of her bleating outrage lasted all the way down the hall to my door.

I slipped my card into the door, came banging into the room and scared Angela nearly to death. She was sitting straight up in bed, wrapped in a blanket right up to her ears, and when I burst in, she screamed and tried to stand up. Her feet got tangled in the blanket and she fell on the bed and rolled off onto the floor.

I helped untangle her, got her on her feet and then asked, "Angela, what's the matter?"

"You startled me, that's all," she said in a quivering voice that almost disappeared as she talked.

"Lord," I said, "if that's how you react when you're startled, what do you do when someone really scares the living lights out of you? Jump out the window?"

"Don't be so silly, Amy. I hate it when you make fun of me. I was sleeping and my stomach's not so hot. I'm okay now, so drop it, will you?"

It was obvious she wasn't all right, but I had to give her time to get calm before I started asking more questions. I couldn't understand it. I had seen her just fifteen minutes ago and she had known I was coming up to the room as soon as I finished my lunch.

She hadn't been sleeping, and she was scared. She was very pale and her breathing was labored. Whatever was worrying her had to be really serious. I gave her a few seconds before I asked her, "Did you hear about what happened to me today?"

"Yes, it was all over the television. I went downstairs and all the TVs were full of terrible pictures of the dead girl, and the murder was all anyone wanted to talk about. I had to get out of there."

Angela started shaking again, so I tried to think of something lighter to take her mind off murder.

"What did you do this morning? I know you decided not to do the Birkebeiner, but I hope you did have some fun."

"I decided to get some fresh air. So I went skiing."

"Were you alone?"

Angela's voice got louder, "Of course I was alone. I'm always alone."

I decided to back off a little. Since her horrible surgery, Angela has gotten thin-skinned and could fly off the handle quite easily. I never got upset with her because I knew what she had gone though and I knew I'd be short-tempered too if it had been me.

"So you went down-hilling," I said. "Did you fall off the chair? No? Well, did you get on a Black Diamond hill by mistake and fall down a lot?"

"I wasn't downhill skiing. I was cross-country skiing."

"Were you on the trail — after the racers left?"

"Amy, you aren't listening. I don't want to talk about it. I'm sorry I went out on the trail. I really didn't want to see anyone, and I never really meant to do anything. I don't know why I had to be there when, when . . ."

My blood turned as cold as Mrs. Smythe-Larson's heart. Angela had been out on the trail. She didn't say where she had started skiing. She could have done what I had done and started part way into the race, arriving at the murder scene before most of the racers did. She could have been there. And she hated Mary Dee and probably knew her bib number. Mary Dee made her do everything for her but breathe, so I knew Angela must have sent for the sign-up sheets, filled them out and gotten the bib with Mary Dee's number on it in return.

She was crying in earnest now and I was suddenly filled with fear that she really might have had something to do with the murder. I looked at her ruined face, now swollen and blotched with tears, and remembered how beautiful she had been before Mary Dee had talked her into that failed and awful cosmetic surgery. It hadn't just ruined her looks. It had ruined Angela's entire life.

Her career as a model was over. And she had been on the way up, getting even national shoots and some interest from New York agencies, inviting her to come out and visit them and bring her portfolio so they could see the kinds of things she had done.

Her blooming romance with a local television anchor had come to an end soon after the operation too. He had tried to continue their relationship but anyone could see he was bothered by Angela's looks. He didn't want to let it bother him, I'll give him that, but the pity that showed every time he looked at her was almost worse than revulsion might have been. Angela soon gave him back his ring, and I know he was relieved, if a little guilty.

The hardest of all was the change in her personality. She had been a very busy and social person with lots of men friends. Now she had become a recluse. She had dropped out of most of her social life and lots of her so-called "friends" had dropped her. Angela had always seemed happy but now was a moody and quite a prickly friend.

Could I blame her if she had tried to shoot Mary Dee? That woman had taken most of what was happy and fulfilling from her life. I was already determined that there was no way in hell I was going to turn her in, and I started thinking of ways I could keep her safe and away from Joe Bear and all the lawmen in Wisconsin.

"Tell me all about it, Angela. I want to help you," I said.

"You can't help me, and I'm not going to talk about it."

"You know you can tell me anything. I certainly am not going to judge you. You know you can trust me."

"I trust you. I don't want to get you involved."

"I am involved. I'm your friend. You know, there are lots of reasons why you've done this. Good legal reasons and I can tell Joe Bear about them. He's the sheriff here and in charge of the murder inquiry. I spent almost the whole day with him. I think he likes me and will really listen to me. So there might not even be any jail time for you to worry about."

"I'm not worried about jail. Why would I worry about jail? I'm worried about getting killed."

"There's no death penalty in Wisconsin, so put that worry right out of your mind. And I think the authorities will agree to hospitalization so you won't have to go to jail."

"Amy, why in the world would I have to go to jail?"

"Well, even justified murder sometimes means a little, tiny bit of jail time, but I know you didn't mean to shoot anyone and anyway you were not in your right mind when you shot at me, thinking I was Mary Dee because I had her bib on. And you shot that girl instead, but it was an accident."

"Amy, don't be nuts. I didn't shoot anyone. Your imagination is in overdrive again. Simmer down."

Maybe murder had turned my brain into dryer lint. Thinking clearly, the idea of reclusive Angela getting up the nerve to shoot anyone was ludicrous. She couldn't even get up the nerve to pour boiling coffee over Mary Dee, which was the least of what that snake deserved for the way she treated her. I was ashamed of myself for my suspicions and said, "I know you're not the violent type, sweetie, but you seem so worried. What are you so afraid of?"

"I don't know what to do. Whether I should turn someone in. Because that person just didn't belong there."

"What person? Where?"

"Well, after you all left, I told you I decided to go skiing by myself."

"And you decided after the racers had all gone by, to try the trail yourself. That shouldn't have scared you. You're the best skier in our group. I still don't know why you didn't enter the race."

"Could we drop that, please? You know why I didn't enter. I hate having people stare at me. Anyway, I decided to try it on my own. And that's when I saw someone."

"Someone you know? Why did that scare you?"

"Because the person was on skis, and all alone at least twenty minutes after most of the other skiers had gone. The trail was empty, except for the two of us."

"Are you sure the person also saw you?"

"Pretty sure,"

"Angela, if you know something, you simply have to tell Sheriff Joe Bear about it. He's full of himself and loves his corny jokes but underneath he seems like a really nice guy. He's also very professional. I trust him to be able to take care of you. You can't do it alone. You could be the next victim if the murderer knows you saw something. You're now the only one who knows this dangerous secret. At the very least, you must tell me the name of the person you saw. That cuts the danger in half."

"No, no I'm not telling anyone yet. There's probably a good reason why that person was out there, and I might get someone into an awful lot of trouble for nothing. It's probably something simple. You know, Amy, you can make small stories into gigantic epics. You're the original drama queen."

"All right. If you don't want to confront the person, let me do it. I'll pretend I had the sighting instead of you."

She thought about it for a moment and then said, "No, I'm not even sure I want to confront anyone. If I decide it's necessary, I'll have to do it myself."

"Oh, you're so stubborn. If this person is involved in any way in this murder, you could be in trouble. If the killer thinks you've seen too much . . . that person has killed once. They say it's usually not as hard to kill a second time."

"Please don't worry. I'm going to be careful. Right now, I don't even think I'll do anything about it. Really, it's no business of mine if someone decided to turn back and not do the race after all. And it could be that the person didn't really see me."

It was getting too late to argue. The big Pirelli party started in just a few minutes. I had to get looking great in a hurry. The bosses at the agency and at Pirellis expected us to be there early to welcome guests. I tried to get Angela to get dressed, but she said she had to take the time to put cold packs on her face to get rid of the tears, the blotches and the swelling. She said she'd come down as soon as she could.

I told her about a million more times to be careful, not to talk to anyone without me at her side. I told her that if she wasn't downstairs in thirty minutes, I'd come back up and get her.

After looking at everything I had brought with me, I pulled out my favorite pair of jeans, the ones that rode low, fit tight and showed off my curves. I added a fairly low-cut sweater and the highest pair of stiletto heels I could find. Not exactly an athletic banquet outfit but heels had always made me feel stronger, more sure of myself. I really needed that tonight. I pulled my hair back and up to the top of my head. That added another couple inches, and I felt the power flowing in.

I gave myself a good looking over in a full-length mirror and wished my favorite wish that I was six feet tall, with long blonde hair. I was really five-foot-three and a half with reddish-brown, curly hair and green eyes. My legs were great, but I had too much bust and lots of freckles. Men told me they thought I was sexy in a cute sort of way. What I wanted to be was glamorous, exotic and super hot in an adult sort of way. Maybe some makeup would help. It'd cover up some of those damn freckles anyway.

Before I left, I called the front desk to see if Ryan Kelly had called. Surely by now he was sorry about our fight and was ready to apologize and let me have my own way. But there were no calls from Ryan. A tiny little cold feeling ran down my spine. He really was playing hard to get. I made up my mind to call him later that night. I didn't have time then, and I was missing a great party. I had to get going.

I turned as I went out the door and said, "Remember, Angela, if you aren't down in thirty minutes, I'm coming back up for you. So start getting ready. Lock the door and don't let anyone in but me."

By the time I left, she was out of bed and starting to look through her closet. She still had a lot of her great modeling wardrobe and the same super body to go with them.

"You have thirty minutes to get ready and then I'll be back up to get you if you're not downstairs," I said as I left.

As I came out of the room, I almost knocked over Stephano, Mama Pirelli's chauffeur. He was a loathsome little toad, and I was convinced he was a member of the Cosa Nostra from Sicily. I was also convinced he'd been listening at our door.

Why would Mama Pirelli want to hear our conversation? Angela and I were as far down the VIP list as we could be and still be included in tonight's festivities.

I turned towards Stephano, and he scuttled away on his little bowed legs just like a large bug. Then he stopped and looked back at me.

I said, "What are you doing out here, Stephano?"

"Is free this country. I go where I like."

"Have you been eavesdropping on us? Tell me right now what you were doing outside our door."

"I don't work for you, missy. I don't have to tell."

"All right. I'm going to call the front desk and ask for security. I'm going to complain about you."

"Senora Pirelli . . . she don't like that."

He was right. Senora Pirelli didn't like anything happening that she hadn't engineered. If I got her precious Stephano in trouble, I'd probably lose my job.

"Okay," I said, "but if I catch you outside our door again, I swear I'll do something to you myself."

He laughed. "What could you do? You too small. You do nothing. People do things to you."

# CHAPTER SEVEN

I HURRIED DOWN TO SCOPE OUT HOW the big Pirelli party was shaping up. It was being held in the huge hall of the Telemark athletic complex. To save some steps, I went outside and walked around the building to the complex. It was snowing heavily, and my hair was powdered white in the few minutes it took me to get there.

The hall was being turned into a Tuscany village by an army of Pirelli people. Heavenly smells of the cooking pasta sauces filled the air. There would be four kinds of sauce and four kinds of Pirelli pasta for dinner plus huge salads, mounds of freshly grated Parmesan and Romano cheeses and loaves of hard-crusted Italian breads. Another long table held dozens of bottles of imported Italian wine—Pinot Grigio, Pinot Noir and Prosecco, a bubbly wine a little like champagne. I hadn't, for once, had my usual gargantuan lunch in hopes that Tiramisu would be the dessert tonight. It was. Mama Pirelli, she who signs the checks, was going all out tonight.

This dinner was by invitation only, but there would also be dozens of church and service club dinners around both Cable and Hayward that were open to all. The Pirelli Party had invited the top two hundred racers plus local notables, television and radio personalities, and the press. They had also invited every elected official from both Minnesota and Wisconsin. Most would come, and anyone up for re-election would be sure to be there.

I left the workers and headed for the pre-dinner cocktail party in Telemark's big lobby. I was enjoying my first cocktail and happily planning an evening of eating, drinking and merriment when out of the corner of my eye I saw one of the Furies approaching. It was Mary Dee, and she was so mad that steam was rising out of her bleached-blond head.

"Stay right there," she screeched. "I've been looking for you. I'm going to kill you, you shitty little runt."

"Ah, Mary Dee," I said, "always the perfect lady."

This naturally made the people around us who knew Mary Dee laugh. This added to her fury, as I had meant it to.

"You cost me a medal, you disgusting little pygmy. You knew I couldn't get a medal without my bib and number. What the hell were you playing at, getting shot at instead of getting my bib to me? I needed it, and you just clowned around instead of doing your job."

"Thank the good lord that my job does not include waiting on you, Mary Dee. But I was trying to do you a favor. I didn't have to do it. And I almost got killed trying. I'm convinced the person who shot at me really wanted to kill you."

That gave her a pause. "Who would want to kill me?"

"Let's me count them up for you," I said. "I'd say nearly everyone who knows you. Every person who has to work directly with you hates you like sin and so do most everyone else in the agency. So do the clients. There's a large number of wives who hate you for borrowing their husbands and returning them damaged beyond repair. Then there are all the discarded boyfriends. Your own family. Even your mother doesn't talk to you. Let's include every salesperson and trades person you've ever dealt with. Did you know your last cleaning lady has a little Voodo doll that looks just like you? And she's stuck that doll all full of pins."

By now we were surrounded by a rather large group of agency and Pirelli people who were roaring with laughter and who now applauded my last line. Mary Dee launched herself towards me, her eyes spinning like someone in need of exorcism. I side-stepped and took off my heels to use as weapons if need be. I heard the sound of *tap, tap, tap* behind me.

"*Basta, basta.* Stop right now both of you. Stop."

I turned and looked into the hooded, snake-like eyes of the Bride of Beelzebub, Mama Pirelli.

"You ruin our nice party, you crazy women."

A simpering smile replaced Mary Dee's mask of fury, and she said, "Oh, Mama Pirelli. I'm so glad you're here. You came just in time to save me from this insane person."

"Basta. I know about you, blondie. All about you. You evil woman. Be quiet."

Then Mama fixed her evil eye on me and said, "And you, little one, you *pazza.*"

Mama Pirelli then *tap, tapped* away, leaving, I thought, a strong smell of sulfur behind her. Probably just my imagination.

Mary Dee gave me a very dirty look but didn't dare say another word. I didn't think until after she had left that she hadn't thought to ask about her jacket. I was glad she hadn't, because I wasn't in any hurry to tell her that it was wrecked. She never would have believed my bunny story.

The party was starting to heat up, and the crowd was getting thicker. I looked at my watch and realized that I had left Angela over thirty minutes ago. I took the stairs in a rush, and when I got to the room, no Angela. There was a note stuck on my pillow with a safety pin. It said, "Mary Dee is looking for you, and she sounded really mad. She didn't get a medal. She also said Mac didn't receive his medal until 1:30 this afternoon. That's a long time for a good skier. Isn't that funny?"

I didn't see anything funny about that, nor did I find it funny that she wasn't here waiting for me. Where could she have gone? I looked around and saw another note labeled

"Amy" on the top of the television. It said, " I can't find my glasses, and you know I need them. I probably left them in the restaurant or maybe in my car. I'll find them and then meet you at the party downstairs—Angela."

Well, my worry eased a little. Before I knew her, I used to be impressed with the lovely, ethereal look she had in close-up shots. It seemed as though she was looking at something beautiful in the distance that no one else could see. Turns out, without her glasses, she couldn't even see the camera clearly. I know she couldn't possibly come to the party without her glasses. She was so near-sighted, she wouldn't be able to recognize anyone.

I went back down to the party. If Angela didn't arrive in a few minutes, I'd go hunt her down. It was possible that she was just putting me off so that she didn't have to come to the party at all. I knew she hated big scenes, especially with a lot of strangers.

I was so busy with my thoughts that I didn't see Mac Larson coming at me until it was too late to run. He seemed a little hot under the old collar, which naturally amused me. I don't know why I always want to laugh at Mac. Maybe it was because he took himself so seriously. He was twenty-eight but one'd swear he was on Social Security.

Maybe it was the way he looked. He always wore an upper-class sneer. In the summers he worked on his tan like he was being paid for it. He bought green and navy plaid pants and wore boat shoes with no socks. You know, retro sixties gear, like he was on his way to a fraternity party. Actually Mac was not bad looking except that he could use a little more chin and a lot more backbone.

"Amy," he said, "what in God's name have you said to Mother? And why do you persist in riling her up?"

"Just a little hobby of mine," I said.

"That's not funny. You know Mother is an old woman. You should have some pity for her. If not, do it for me and for your own future."

"My future?" I said blankly. "What does needling your sainted Mother have to do with my future? I was hoping it'd keep her the hell out of my future."

"Well, you're ruining our chances."

"Chances for what?"

"Of becoming a team, partners together in a great romance, and a great endeavor that will make my success in politics a sure thing. But for all that to happen, we're going to need Mother's approval. And her money, naturally."

"Mac," I said, "I haven't got the time to argue with you about our non-existent romance. I'm looking for Angela. Have you seen her?"

Mac looked surly and launched into another one of his pet subjects: People Who Matter and People Who Don't.

"No, I have not seen her, and I can't imagine why you are looking for her. There are so many other people at this party who are more interesting and more—ah—influential for you to spend time with. Think about your career and, more importantly, *my* career."

I looked at him, and I could tell he had absolutely no idea what a pompous frog he was, so there was no advantage or fun in pointing out that fact to him. I also knew it might end by my disfiguring him or getting thrown out of the party. Besides, I could use him.

"Well, Mac, I've got to find her, and I don't want to go poking around dark places by myself. I need you to come with me."

"Oh, all right. I have to get my jacket and gloves though. I'm not going to catch a cold for Angela."

I ran up to our room to get my outdoor jacket, and while I was there I made a quick inventory of Angela's clothes. I could see that her boots were gone and so was her jacket. I raced back downstairs and met Mac. Together we went to the hotel dining room. We walked the length of the room looking, but no Angela.

I stopped at the front desk and asked the hostess if she had noticed a young woman looking for something. She replied, "Do you mean that girl with the funny face? Yes, she was here looking for her glasses. She looked all over, but we didn't have them."

My heart ached for Angela. That was all people saw when they looked at her. Her funny face. "Did you see where she went when she left you?" I asked.

"No I didn't but she had her outdoor clothes on. And she was pulling her hat on as she left. I'll bet she was going outside."

Over Mac's grumbles, we started outside. It was colder now with a real blizzard building up. The hundreds of cars in the big parking lot wore dollops of fluffy snow like whipped cream.

Angela had a little, red Ford about ten years old. I told Mac, and we split up to look row by row for her car. It was hard going because we had to stop when we came to a red car and brush off enough snow so that we could see what make it was. It felt like I had looked at about three hundred cars and was soaked through when Mac finally yelled. "I think this is it, Amy. Come over here."

It was Angela's car, and it was empty. The trunk lid was up and the trunk had started to fill with snow. There were a lot of scuffle marks all around the back of the car, and big and small boot prints.

I moved around to the side of the car and tried the front door. It opened so I knew Angela had been here. She never left her car unlocked. I got in and looked around. There on the dashboard of the car were her glasses. She wouldn't have left without her glasses either. Angela had to be in big trouble.

I pulled out my cell phone and called 911. The woman on the other end didn't seem to be as worried as I wanted her to be. I told her the situation, and she asked if there was any evidence of foul play such as blood, broken windows, or a forced car door.

I had to admit there was nothing like that. But I added, "The trunk was left up and her glasses were on top of the dash. She wouldn't have left willingly without her glasses."

"I'll notify the Cable police, ma'am. They'll send someone out to investigate. But this is a very busy weekend, and they're stretched thin."

In the background I could hear Mac bleating. "You are making a fool of yourself and me. Have you lost your mind? Hang up the phone and let's get back inside where it's warm."

I yelled back, "Go find the head of Security and tell him to meet me out here in the parking lot."

I raced for the Telemark lobby and streaked by the startled guests enjoying the cocktails and canapés of the Pirelli party and hurled myself up the stairs to our room. I dumped my purse on the bed and searched frantically until I found Joe's card. I called the number and, thank all the gods there are, he answered.

I said, "Joe, it's Amy Connolly. Please come right away. Angela's disappeared and you have to trust me. She's in real trouble. She knew something and wouldn't tell me and now she's gone. Her car is open, the trunk lid was up and it looked like there had been some sort of struggle."

"Stay inside, Amy. Stay with people. I'll be there in seven minutes and I'll bring all the help I can find."

I bumped into Mac almost outside my door, and he whined, "What have you done now?"

"I got some help. Until they get here, we can start looking. Have you got a flashlight?"

"It's in my car. I don't think any of this is necessary, Amy. You're just in a panic mode."

"I am, Mac, and if you don't help me you're going to be in hurt mode. Get your damn flashlight and meet me by Angela's car."

I ran back outside and by now I could hear the sirens. They were coming from two directions, south from Cable and north from Hayward. Real help was coming and coming fast.

When Joe got there, he was not happy to see me outside, still standing by Angela's car, but he didn't give me heat. This was another point in the mental score card I was keeping in his favor. He didn't waste time telling me not to do something I was already in the middle of doing. Instead he asked for background. I gave him the bare bones of why I thought Angela was in trouble, and he moved the deputies out to search.

Soon we could see lights, flickering in the dark, all around the main Telemark buildings, radiating farther and farther out from the center. There were officers from both Cable and Hayward, two State Patrol cars and a Lac Courte Oreille Reservation squad car was just pulling in.

Joe came back, turned to Mac and said, "Get Miss Connolly back inside."

"Look here, officer," Mac said. "I don't think you appreciate who you are dealing with. I don't like you giving me orders, and I don't like your tone of voice."

"And I don't like you, period." Joe said. "Now get the hell out of here before I cuff you and take you in."

Mac slunk off like a scolded puppy. I turned to go inside and as I did I saw something funny. The lights on the downhill runs were all turned off but I could see the chair lift moving.

"Joe, look. The chair lift. It's moving."

"Okay. Get back inside now, Amy. It's okay."

"No, no . . . it's not okay. The chair lift is not supposed to be running tonight. It was to be shut off, canceled for the Birkebeiner Winner's party. And they would never run the chairs without all the lights being on and — see — the hill is dark. That is so unsafe. So why is the chair lift running?"

# Chapter Eight

W<small>E ALL RAN TOWARDS THE LIFT.</small> As we got closer we could see a bundle of what looked like rags, slumped over in one of the chairs, going slowly around and around. Joe was calling his deputies as he ran and soon an army of lights was heading our way. Joe headed straight for the little hut that housed the lift machinery. It was locked tight with a big, business-like Yale lock. He didn't wait for someone to find a key; he took out his gun and shot the lock off. Then he asked for an experienced lift operator to take over, slow the lift down, wait for the right chair to come by and then slowly stop it.

As most of the young people in Sawyer and Bayfield counties had worked for Telemark at some time during high school or college, an operator wasn't hard to find. Joe chose one of the volunteers and told him to go gently, so that there would be no chance of more damage to whatever was in that chair. He sent some of his crew back to patrol the area. The others were told to control the crowds pouring out of the lodge and surrounding chalets, alerted by the sound of the sirens and gunfire.

I wanted to get as close as I could to the ski lift without getting in the way of the police. I raced toward the lift with Mac right behind me, trying to grab my jacket and slow me down, whining about how cold he was, how stupid I was behaving and begging me to stop and go back inside.

"It's your own fault you're cold," I screamed back at him. "You came out tonight in a raincoat instead of a parka. Now leave me alone. I know that moving lift means trouble, and I'll bet it has something to do with Angela's disappearance."

Mac couldn't have stopped me now with a Tomahawk cruise missile. I squeezed in as close as I could to the lift and waited, sick with dread. It was very dark and cold waiting for the right chair to appear on the lift platform and stop. First the bundle went way up to the top of the slope and then slowly, slowly descended. They were being very careful not to shake the bundle and possibly dislodge it. If they did, it would have a very long way to fall to very frozen ground.

The right chair finally swung down and stopped in place on the loading platform. I still couldn't see much of anything. What I could see looked like a big, shiny, elongated snowball. It was mainly white but I could see some color shining through. Bright, bright blue. It was Angela. I knew it was, knew it to be true, although all I could see was that tiny glimpse of blue. Angela's bright blue jacket.

A wail of a siren announced that the police emergency crew had arrived. They brought their ambulance close to the lift, took out a gurney and slowly, carefully placed the shiny ice bundle down on it.

And then it seemed like nothing much was happening. I expected they would start removing all the snow, ice, and frozen clothing. Instead they were just brushing the bundle, where I thought her face must be, with a small, soft brush like the kind women use to brush on powder.

I raced to Joe's side and grabbed his arm. "Joe, is it Angela? Is she going to be okay?"

"I don't know who it is yet, and it's going to take awhile to make sure the person is still alive. I know you want to help, but you can help the most by getting out of the way. If it's your friend and she can be saved, these guys will save her. All emergency personnel and police in climates like ours have extensive training in the care of freezing victims. They know what to do."

I faded back a few feet and listened and waited. I still didn't see much activity from the first aid crew. Why weren't they getting Angela out of the cold and putting her into something warm? What were they waiting for?

Joe started barking orders. "Keep the motor on the ambulance running but turn off the heater and open the doors and windows. When it's just barely warm, let us know."

The workers keep on brushing snow slowly, slowly off the bundle. Now I could see it was a body, but oh such a terrible looking, icy body. Could anyone live through this?

When the driver yelled that the ambulance was at optimum temperature, the crew cautiously walked the gurney to it and put it in. I could see them start to take off what they could of Angela's clothes and then wrap her in warm blankets. As these blankets got cold and wet, they replaced them. And then more clothes got removed.

I found out later that what they were doing, and doing expertly, was called passive warming. A freezing victim can't be warmed up fast. People used to try and warm a frozen person or body part as fast as they could and this was often fatal. Go very slowly and do no harm is the primary rule of passive warming.

A sound like a crazed eggbeater filled the air and a helicopter appeared in the sky directly over the ski hill. It started nosing and then sinking down. As soon as it stopped, a crew got out and raced for the ambulance and reappeared soon with the patient on the gurney, loaded her up and took off again, heading south to Hayward.

The whole procedure seemed to take less than a minute. Before they left, Joe gestured to one of his deputies to get on the copter and go with the crew. They were on their way to the hospital.

I felt better knowing that Angela was on her way to Hayward Memorial. It was a Class A Emergency Hospital, very state-of-the-art and practically new. And the staff was wonderful, helpful and kind. I knew this because I had been their guest practically every time I'd been near Hayward. Even when I wasn't doing anything dangerous, like skiing, I had accidents like slipping on the ice, sticking a wine opener into my palm instead of the bottle, and spraining my ankle dumping a canoe in Little Joe, some rapids on the Brule. They knew me on a first name basis at Hayward Memorial.

Because all the police in Northern Wisconsin were on alert during the Birkebeiner, it really had taken only minutes for the helicopter to get there. All vacations and days off were typically canceled for the race, and when they were through with their regular shifts, most first aid workers headed out as volunteers during the Birkebeiner. There are over 2,000 volunteers working before, during and after the race. It was so lucky that they were here tonight for Angela.

I grabbed Joe as he went by, and I didn't have to say a word. He knew what I wanted to know.

"I'm sorry, Amy I don't know yet. Before they got there, the paramedics tried but couldn't find a pulse. I knew that doesn't always mean the person is dead. Whether or not she'll make it depends on how hard she was hit before the perp put her in that chair."

"She was hit?"

Joe said, "I'm afraid so. I could see a big injury to the back of her head. Her chances also depend on how long she was out there. Can you give me some idea of the time? It's important so try and make the timing as close as you can."

I tried to figure it out. "I waited almost thirty minutes for her at the party and when she didn't come, I went back up to see what she was doing but found her and her jacket and boots gone. I got my outdoor stuff on and went to look for her. Mac followed me out, and I got him to help. The whole thing — finding the car and knowing she was in trouble took about six or seven minutes. Add my time getting a message to you and your time getting here, another seven or eight minutes."

"We have to add more minutes getting the body from the lift and into the ambulance, time for the copter to come down and for them to get your friend into it."

"Is it too long? Doesn't she have a chance?"

Joe ignored my questions while he called the time in to the hospital. Then he turned to me and said, "I don't know if it's too long but our times together are about twenty-five minutes and what we don't know is how long she was out here before you missed her. If it was the entire thirty minutes, plus ours, well, fifty-five minutes is a long time to be out in this kind of weather. It's about ten degrees below zero right now and still dropping."

I was shaking so hard with fear I could barely speak. "Does all that time mean they can't save her or, if they do, she won't be the same?"

"Not necessarily. We did get a real break. The vicious punk who put your friend in that chairlift was, luckily, a moron. He packed snow all around her as tight as he could, probably figuring that would make her die faster."

"Oh, my God," I said. "This murderer is really brutal and vicious. He really wanted to kill her."

"He probably did want her dead but actually," Joe said, "it had just the opposite effect. Snow is a terrific insulator so what he really did was put another heavy jacket over her. His stupidity might have saved her life."

By now I was a little happier but still shivering uncontrollably, and Joe noticed. "There's nothing you can do right now, Amy, and you should get in out of the cold. Try to remember everything you can that Angela told you."

Dan Clark, head of the hotel Security, had arrived on the scene and was waiting to talk to Joe. Joe asked him what had taken him so long to get there. The young, good-looking, blond giant of a man, who was known to be always smiling and one of the friendliest guys in Northern Wisconsin, tonight looked murderous.

"I'll tell you why. Some idiot called us and told us there had been a big accident out at the Telemark Airport, and I raced out there with most of my crew to find nothing. By the time we got back, you had arrived. If I find that guy, I'll cream him."

Joe said, "Cool it, Dan. I know the snafu wasn't your fault. You're doing a great job with security at Telemark. I'd love to have you working for me in Bayfield. Or you'd be great in the Tribal Police. Sure you can't find some good Ojibwa ancestor in your family background?"

Dan laughed and his usual affable mood was back. Joe looked at me and said, "Amy, did you tell the guy you were with to call for help? He knew where the emergency was."

I looked around before I answered, but Mac was long gone. "Of course he knew where the trouble was. I told him to call Security when I went up to my room to call you. I told him we needed help here, in this parking lot. He must have thought my panic was a joke."

"Nice guys you hang around with," Joe said sarcastically.

"Well," I said, "I'm hoping they're about to get a lot better."

Joe laughed and gave me a look that melted my bones. "Listen, I want to know exactly what Angela said to you that made you think she had some idea of who the murderer is. I've got to talk to some people here and then I'm going to head down to Hayward and the hospital. I'd like you to ride with me and tell me all you can remember on the way."

"Oh, I'm so glad. I want to be there when Angela wakes up. She will wake up, won't she, Joe?"

Joe just shook his head so I went on hurriedly, "I'll tell you everything I remember but it was fragmented. I'll go back to the room and get my things and meet you by the front doors."

I had grabbed my purse and started out my bedroom door when Mac appeared in the hall. He was breathing hard and looked pale. For the first time since I've known him, his hair was mussed up. Finally Angela's plight had gotten through to him, I thought. He does have a heart after all.

"Oh, God . . . this is awful, Amy. Tragic. I'm in a complete state of shock and I don't know what to do."

"Gosh, Mac. I'm surprised but happy to know how concerned you are about Angela."

"Angela? Who cares about Angela? Anyone stupid enough to go out in the dark to look for a pair of glasses probably got just what she deserved. She'll either live or she won't live, so her problems are solved. But what about me? Can't you see how this affects me? I can't be involved in a sordid crime. It could easily hurt my public image. There's always a lot of collateral damage, you know, when there's a crime. There are really lots of victims."

I couldn't believe it but I had to because he was saying it. I realized suddenly that Mac's traits I had always thought of as funny and kind of sad were anything but. This was a monster I couldn't wait to be rid of.

I pushed him out of my way, locked my door and ran down the stairs to the lobby. I could see the squad car idling in front of the door. Joe was talking on the radio so I tried to slide in quietly and not slam the door.

Joe finished and said, "Well, did you ask your friend why he sent the Telemark troops out to the airport?"

"No. I knew he wouldn't have a good answer. He might have forgotten. Or he might have been mad because I ordered him to call. He's a totally selfish waste of space."

I made a little joke of it but I was really shaken by what Mac had said. It was spooky when someone you think you know turns out to be someone quite different. And I realized something else. I was now more than a little afraid of Mac Larson.

He had the single-minded selfishness I'd heard murderers need. To kill someone, you had to think your affairs and your safety were more important than another's life. Maybe Mac wasn't just a conceited, little ninny. Maybe ineffectual, mommy-bossed Mac could be a killer.

But I couldn't think of a good reason why he'd want to kill Mary Dee. And that was the crime that had led to Angela's accident. I was certain of that. Of all the people at Pylon and Voss Agency or at Pirelli's Perfect Pasta, Mac was the one closest to Mary Dee. Or maybe I should say he was one of the few who could stand her. They had or maybe still did date occasionally. So Mac would have no reason to want her dead.

Of course, Mrs. Smythe-Larson, Mac's mother, hated Mary Dee. But if everyone whom Mac's mama hated had to be killed, the Upper Midwest would be littered with bodies.

As we started for Hayward and the hospital, I told Joe everything I could think of that might throw light on the first murder and the attempted murder of Angela. I was no longer worried about getting friends in trouble. I figured if they were innocent, they'd be okay. I was too worried and too angry about Angela. I wanted the murderer found.

Joe was firing questions at me so fast I could hardly keep up. My family would never believe this. I'd finally met someone who talked faster than I did.

Joe said, "What exactly did she say? Was it a man or a woman? Where was she and why? Was she surprised to see this person?"

"As near as I can remember, and I know this is important, she said she had seen someone where they shouldn't have been. Her words were 'that person just didn't belong there' and she was puzzled."

"Where was she when she saw the person and was it someone she knew?"

"She decided to go skiing by herself after the race started and we'd all left. She was out on the big trail. What she had seen didn't scare her until later when she heard about the murder. But she didn't know what to do about it. She was afraid of getting someone in trouble. I'm sure that means she knew the person. And she was very careful not to say he or she so I have no idea if she saw a man or a woman."

"Did you ask her to tell you all about it, who it was and why it worried her?"

"I begged her to tell me or to tell you, but she wasn't ready. She said it wouldn't be fair to get me involved. I got the feeling she was getting up her nerve to confront the person herself."

Joe went into a little rant about people who thought they should do their own police work and ended up dead. I looked so horrified at the word "dead" that he stopped and tried to tell me that he didn't mean Angela.

"Don't look like that, Amy. I didn't mean your friend. Forget I said that and concentrate on anything, even the smallest detail, that Angela said or that you sensed."

"This is just a hunch, Joe, but I think she saw someone who was a skier, a contestant. The person was out on the trail but far back even from the last wave of skiers. It was someone, I think, who she thought should be pretty much at the front

62

of the pack. If she had just seen a friend, she would have said something, made herself known. But if she saw a good skier, one who should be a lot further down the trail and wasn't, she'd be suspicious."

"Did she say if the other person had seen her?"

"She didn't say specifically. At first she said yes and then later she wasn't sure the other person hadn't noticed her."

We covered the twenty miles or so to Hayward in less, quite a bit less, than fifteen minutes. I had always wanted to be in a police car, screaming down a highway with lights blazing and sirens going at full decibels. It wasn't at all fun tonight because I was worried and because of all the idiots on the highway who kept getting in our way. My respect for lawmen increased a thousand-fold. They had to be fearless. And damn good drivers. If I got another scary ride with Joe like this, I'd want him to stop and ticket every bozo that refused to pull over and get out of our way. On a perfect date, he'd let me hand out the tickets.

# CHAPTER NINE

I SAT IN THE WAITING ROOM of the Hayward Hospital emergency room for what seemed like hours without news. Joe was really busy on his cell phone arranging for guards for Angela from the Sawyer County sheriff's office and trying to run his murder investigation from a distance.

I could see a crowd outside the doors of the ER as he came in and out. It was full of media people waiting for some news. The Birkebeiner attracted skiers and press from all over the world. Now the murder and attempted murder had brought a horde more. Added to all the color and crowds and festivities of the race, the crimes had made the area the hottest news story in the world.

I spent my time watching the flow of accidents that always happen when you had a huge crowd like they did for the Birkebeiner. Figure about two to three family members or onlookers for each of the five to six thousand skiers, and you'd have around twenty thousand outsiders in town. Tonight's ER visitors included skiers who, once the euphoria and liquor had worn off, felt they might have broken something after all. Add lots of frozen fingers and toes and even more people complaining about colds. The most miserable patient was a young boy who had eaten so much pasta for two nights at spaghetti dinners that I could see his distended stomach from where I sat.

Two deputies from Sawyer arrived and joined Joe. He gave them orders for guarding Angela and when he was done he came over and asked me how I was. I could see he was busy and anxious to keep moving so I didn't bother him with my fears.

Finally the charge nurse came out to the waiting room and told me that they had started Angela on an active warming system. I learned this involved an infusion of warmed IV fluids that started at a temperature just barely past cold and were slowly, by degree, getting warmer and warmer. She warned me that it could take hours before we knew if Angela was going to live.

The active warming treatment seemed to go on forever as I waited. I was miserable, worried and so very lonely. I was left with no one to share my worries or feelings. I felt abandoned. When I thought about it, I realized that it was Ryan I needed and really wanted. Everything would end happily if he were here. Ryan was the only guy I knew willing to listen to me talk about my feelings until I feel better. He always makes me feel safe and loved and happy.

Finally, the doors to the stabilization room opened and a very young and tired doctor came out. He asked me if I was related to Angela. I knew he wouldn't give me any information unless I was a relative, so I said I was her sister.

He had good news and bad news. "Angela is still alive but just barely. The active warming we've been doing kept your sister alive but it's not enough. We're going to start something else now, an abdominal flush."

I said, "What is that? Is it dangerous?"

"There's always some danger with every procedure, but there's more danger in not doing it. A simplified explanation is that an abdominal flush involves creating a small hole in the patient's side and putting a tube right into her body. This allows us to force warm water right into the abdominal cavity. We make another small hole in the other side to let the water out."

I wanted him to tell me if she would live. He shook his head. "We should know in the next two hours whether we're able to save your sister or not. I'm sorry that I won't have a definitive answer until then. I know how worried you are."

He left and I was alone again to think of the holes they were poking in Angela's body. If she lived, she'd have two more scars to add to the awful ones she already had. She'd hate that but I prayed blessings on the new scars. Let them save her life, please.

Memories flooded back. The first time I could remember Angela saying something funny was during an interminable meeting about an upcoming fashion campaign in which she was to star. She said something so softly I just barely caught it. It was more than funny; it was smack on the money funny. I had looked over at Angela, and she winked at me. I had a new friend.

We started doing things together, movies, an occasional concert and bar hops. Mary Dee, of course, accused me of hanging out with Angela to meet guys. Which was true. Before all her operations, she was a real good-looking man magnet. Ryan was gone for weeks at a time, getting his law degree at Harvard. So I needed dates. Oh, nothing serious. Just something to keep me amused until Ryan came home or I went to Cambridge for a weekend. Angela did get me lots of dates. But she was also great to be with, clever, smart, irreverent, and sarcastic. And best of all, she was wickedly funny with a bite, a little bit of a mean edge.

There was nobody I'd rather spend time with than a person who shared my sense of the often-ridiculous things that happened in the world of advertising, especially the hyper-nonsense of a fashion photo shoot. Angela and I were often together at them.

A typical shoot included the master photographer, a film loader, a scene lighter, a dresser, a make-up person, and the model. Added to that were assistants, every agency person who had the slightest reason to be there, and clients watching their money disappear. Plus there was always a good caterer because shoots often last a full day and into the evening and it was vital to keep up the morale. The clients expect it and frankly I thought the food was the only reason most showed up.

After Angela's botched operation, I hoped I'd helped her to want to live. She hadn't just lost her looks, friends, and fiancé. She had also lost a lot of her plans for the future with the absence of her big modeling paychecks. With them, she had helped her aging grandparents and she was gradually working on her college education. Without the money, she was devastated and depressed and poor.

Perhaps worst of all for Angela was her lost beauty. She had gone from being gorgeous to someone who made people wince when they saw her. I spent a lot of time trying to get her to see that her looks were only a small part of why she was beautiful and why I valued her friendship.

I told her, "You're so much more of a person than this skin-deep stuff. This operation hasn't damaged your brain, hasn't destroyed the core of you that makes you such a great human being."

I'd said these things and lots more as we sat in her little apartment and waited for all the stitches to come out, for all her scars to fade a little. Gradually she fought back. It took a lot of courage for her to leave the apartment, to let people see her ruined face. But she did it and got herself back to work—different work—and somewhat functioning. She had changed though; she'd gotten bitter, brittle. Her conversation was laced with more trash-talk, quite a lot of resentful bitching and her jokes had turned dark. Who could blame her?

The night went on and on, the way terrible nights do. The doors to the ER, where Angela fought to live, stayed shut. No one came out to tell me things would be fine or not to worry. I finally fell asleep and I must have slept for a couple hours because the night was turning into morning when I woke up. I walked outside the front door of the hospital and stood shivering in the cold. Some nights in northern Wisconsin and Minnesota, stars were so bright you could read by them. Tonight all I could see was black sky. At dawn, as the sky lightened, and on the edges of the black, some fingers of gray crept in like tendrils of smoke. The stars that were usually so close and clear up here were gone.

A nurse came out, hugging her arms to keep warm. "The doctor wants to talk to you. He'll be out in a minute. When he's done, please stop by the desk. We need to get some personal information on your sister and about her health insurance. And it's critical now that we find out about her next-of-kin."

When she said that, I just knew Angela was dead. I felt my stomach fall. My knees weakened. I must have looked like I was about to die myself because the nurse quickly said. "No, no your sister's alive. I didn't mean to scare you. The doctor will tell you all about her condition in a minute. Come back inside before we have you for a patient too."

I noticed that the young doctor looked very tired and seemed to have aged overnight. He was taking off his surgical cap as he walked slowly towards me. He said. "Your sister is going to live. It's too soon to tell exactly how much damage was done to her lungs because of the freezing. Right now she does have a bad case of pneumonia but we expected that. We just don't know how bad it is. We're going to send her to St. Luke's in Duluth this morning. They have equipment in their pulmonary unit we don't. You can see her for a moment now. She's still sedated so she probably won't know you're there, but I hope it'll make you feel better. Bayfield is sending their helicopter to transfer Angela and I'm going with her."

My throat was so tight I couldn't say my thanks. So I just grabbed the doctor and hugged him. Unshaven, with mussed hair, and tired eyes, he looked like a saint to me.

Joe arrived just in time to hear the last of the doctor's speech. He added, "And so am I with two deputies from my office. We're putting a twenty-four/seven watch on Angela, so you can relax, Amy. She'll be safe, I promise."

"Can't I go with her? She'll need a familiar face when she wakes up. She's going to be so scared."

"Sorry, but police procedure says I have to treat you as a possible suspect. Wait. Before you get all wound up, I'm pretty sure you didn't do it. But you're going to have to be treated just like the others in your group until we get all the times and alibis sorted out. Anything else might be considered favoritism on my part for you."

Well, what was so wrong with that? I craved a little favoritism from Joe who even looked good with black stubble and tired eyes, after our very long night. I naturally wanted to launch into a long complaint. But I figured now was the time to show Joe the softer, more reasonable and, hopefully, more darling side to my nature. So I agreed demurely. I was feeling incredibly happy knowing Angela was alive and, I hoped, on her way to being completely okay. I could afford to be generous.

I went in to say my good-byes to her. She looked less gray and more like herself than she had before, but her breathing sounded horrible. Great rattling noises came from her lungs, and she seemed to struggle for each breath.

When the helicopter came, I went outside and watched them load Angela, Joe, and the deputies aboard and take off before I returned to the ER to talk to the nurse at the charge desk. I gave her all the information I knew about Angela—age, where she worked, and what kind of hospitalization insurance the agency had. When I got to the next-of-kin, I knew I needed help.

"Angela isn't married and our parents are both dead. Our grandparents raised her. I would've called them before but they're very old and very dependent on Angela. I didn't want to bother them until I had something concrete to tell them. And the big problem is they speak hardly any English. I'm going to need some help. We'll need a Czechoslovakian translator."

I suppose the nurse thought it was strange I didn't know more about Angela's or my own grandparents. Or why hadn't I learned a little Czech? That was one of the troubles with my lies. I said them before I had time to flesh out a story.

"Well," the nurse said, "I'll need more information including their names, an address, and their phone number."

Luckily I did know the phone number so I gave her that and added, "Their name is Krajak, of course, and I'd tell you their first names but, honestly, they are so hard to pronounce it's better to just call them Grandma and Grandpa."

That sweet nurse probably thought I was insane when she found out the next day that Angela's grandparent's first names are simply Joseph and Maria.

Mike, the deputy Joe had left to watch over me came looking for me. I told him my language problem and he told me not to worry but to write out what I wanted to say and they would get it translated and get the message delivered to the Krajaks.

Mike said, "This part of Wisconsin is full of immigrants from Eastern Europe. We should be able find a good Czech translator quickly. And we'll get some help from the Duluth police or more likely the Minnesota State Patrol to get a translator to be with the grandparents. If they can't find a Czech translator fast locally, they'll use the National Law Enforcement Translation Service."

I sat down to write out a message for the Krajaks, and it was tricky because I wanted to tell them a little about how Angela had gotten sick without going into anything about crazed killers or how close she had come to dying. That could wait until they saw her and knew she was going to live before they got all the grim background information. I finally just told them that Angela had stayed out in the cold too long, which was no lie. And that she had caught a very bad cold.

It was after ten Sunday morning when Mike the deputy and I left the hospital and headed north towards Cable and Telemark. It was still cold, way below zero, and it was snowing harder. Even some of the big pines swayed a bit towards the ground they were so loaded with snow. I was happy anyway. My friend was alive, and that made the day beautiful.

A long line of cars sped by us, heading for the Cities. The race was over for the race participants. I wondered what was happening with the Pirelli party. This race was far from over for all of us.

"What's going to happen now, Mike? Are we going to be allowed to go home today? What's everybody been doing since I left last night? Are you any closer to knowing who did this to Angela?"

"Well, you know Ms. Connolly, I'm just a fill-in deputy right now for Sheriff Bear. I retired a couple years ago, and I just get called in when they need extra help. I'm not really in on what's been going on at Telemark because I've been at the hospital since last night. I do know that your group is still there and have all volunteered to stay until they get all your statements taken."

"How long will that take?"

"It could take a day or a couple days. The group, I understand, has been moved into one wing of the hotel segregated from the rest of the guests. That's really all I know."

*Oh, wonderful,* I thought. Soon I'll be in quarantine with a bunch of angry, scared, bored people and, worst of all, I would be shut up with a murderer. I felt as if I were about to star in a Bad Girls in Prison movie where crazed prisoners, vicious guards and a lecherous warden were all stalking me, the innocent little heroine. Well, I had complained often enough about my boring life. Now I was in the middle of a real murder mystery. One I was sure I could solve, of course. But it wasn't as much fun as I always thought it would be. Hadn't been fun at all. It had been sad and scary.

"Oh, Deputy Mike? Who'll be in charge while Joe's gone?"

"That's going to be Deputy Inga Johnson. She's in charge."

Now I was really depressed.

# CHAPTER TEN

I SPENT THE TIME ON THE RIDE BACK to Telemark trying out my interrogation skills on Deputy Mike. He refused to answer any of my questions even though I asked them in several different and very creative ways.

He said, "Joe told me you were a caution, Ms. Connolly. He said you were more curious and clever than a mess of meerkats. Now, you just relax. He'll be back tonight, and you can ask him then."

It was certainly a good sign that Joe had been talking about me but the comparison to meerkats I could have done without. I decided it was no use wasting good questions on Mike. Joe had told him not to tell me anything.

When we got back to Telemark I was sent to the Chippewa Room, a large meeting room that was being used as a dining and gathering space for the Pirelli party. A general clamor and greetings arose from my friends who came over to me in a rush to find out what had happened to Angela, and if I knew anything more about the murder.

In the midst of all this excitement, I felt a cold breeze. In flew Brunhilde, Viking Queen of the Frigid, a.k.a Deputy Inga Johnson. She proceeded to lay down the law.

She warned me that if I wasn't in my room, I was expected to be in the Chippewa Room and nowhere else. I was not allowed the run of the complex. If I needed to go outdoors, I would have the company of an armed escort, either a deputy or one of the Telemark security guards. It was obvious that Deputy Johnson felt no need of wasting time on a trial, with judge and jury, to find me guilty.

I was willing to bet that before Joe came back, the Ice Queen would try to get me into prison clothes. Large, baggy prison clothes with snarled hair and no makeup either.

I wanted to tell her to try a painful anatomical procedure on herself but decided to give her no reason to get me into trouble with Joe. I just smiled sweetly and thanked her for all her helpful information. Then I thanked her for being so solicitous about my well-being. This seemed to make her thin little lips almost disappear. She had expected trouble and hadn't gotten any from me. Now she couldn't punish me or make my life hell. What a disappointment for her. Feeling victorious, I headed for my room and a long nap.

When I awoke, it was afternoon and well into acceptable drinking time. And because this was a gathering of advertising people, I knew there would be a fully stocked bar in the Chippewa Room.

I got dressed in a flash and headed down. As I stood pouring myself a drink, a long white arm hooked its way around my neck. I turned and looked into the beautiful, green, slightly dizzy, eyes of Virginia Pylon. Virginia, the wife of my boss, agency president and creative director Chuck Pylon was laughing, and, as I was nose to nose with her, I took in a breath of almost pure alcohol and felt suddenly as though I'd been drinking all day too.

"Where've you been, Munchkin?" Virginia breathed. "I've been looking all over for you to personally congratulate you on a job well done."

"Oh," I said preening a bit. "You're probably talking about our latest series of ads for the Galleria. Well, modesty aside, I have to admit we did do a rather good job on that campaign."

"Ads?" Virginia scoffed, "I never pay any attention to any of them. I've had to listen to Chuck blow off about creativity and advertising for so many years, I turn off my ears at the first hint. My mind just zonks out until I can tell he's winding down. Then I ask him about the media plan and relax. He'll go on for another hour on the stupid buys of the media department, the incredible bad research he gets from marketing and the penny pinching from client nerds. I tell you, Munchkin, being a good wife is hard work."

"I can see that," I said, "but what were you congratulating me for?"

"Well, for the almost shooting of that hag, Mary Dee. I hate Mary Dee, you know. And that makes me mad because I've never hated anyone before in my life."

"Lots of people hate her, Virginia. But I didn't shoot her. I can't take credit for a job I didn't have anything to do with."

"Yeah, but you really told her off. Made her look stupid. I loved that bit about her cleaning lady hating her enough to make little fetish dolls of her."

"Thanks. But why do you hate her?"

Virginia moved in closer, tottering a bit on her four-inch stilettos. "I hate her because of Chuck. Because of what she's done to him."

I said, "To Chuck?. Chuck isn't involved with Mary Dee. You can put that worry right out of your mind."

"I know that," Virginia laughed as she stood weaving from side to side, held up only by her arm around my neck. I felt as though I'd gone to sea during a thick, alcoholic fog in a very unstable boat.

"I mean, fear of sounding big-headed aside, Munchkin, I know I'm great looking and I know Chuck's crazy about me." She hiccupped and said, "I'd never say anything that conceited usually but I might have taken a tad too much drink today. But I'm not jealous. God, Mary Dee's no competition that way. But she's done something to worry him. She's put some sort of horrible hex on him and . . ."

Virginia went on muttering softly as she started to slide slowly towards the floor. I tried to hold her up, but I was six inches shorter than she was and I was losing ground fast. Through a tangle of her honey blonde hair, I could see Chuck Pylon coming our way as fast as he could.

"Hi, honey," he said carefully, "I thought I'd spotted you."

There was no answer from Virginia.

"Honey?"

I could feel Virginia slide down another few inches. Some very loud snores were coming from deep within her throat.

Chuck got on her other side and we slid and lifted her towards a big, deep chair. We lowered her carefully and then looked at each other ruefully across his now totally unconscious wife. I was embarrassed. I really loved Chuck, in a father-figure sort of way, of course. I mean, he was really old. He must be over forty. But he was kind and creative and a great boss and I hated seeing him and Virginia, who I like a lot too, in trouble.

Chuck patted my hand. "Well, Amy . . . you've had quite a Saturday."

"It's been terrible. But Angela's still alive and I hope will be better soon."

"I heard that and I'm glad. Did she wake up? Does she remember anything? As soon as she can talk, we'll be out of this nightmare and know who's responsible. Then my wife can start to feel better."

Chuck turned and gave Virginia a fond, worried glance.

"You can't think that Virginia had anything to do with any of this, Chuck."

Chuck looked totally surprised and then started to chuckle. "I knew you were super imaginative Amy. That's why I hired you. But don't let it run away with your good sense. Of course I know Virginia didn't have anything to do with the crime. She's unhappy because of me. And, uh, my relationship with Mary Dee."

"Mary Dee? Oh, Chuck I'm going to be sick. Mary Dee doesn't have relationships. She has victims. Tell me you didn't get involved."

"I didn't mean to imply anything personal, like sex, Amy. Makes me nauseated to even think of sex with her."

"So what's she got to do with Virginia being unhappy? Mary Dee couldn't possibly do anything to hurt the two of you. You're the most together couple I know."

I looked at Chuck and suddenly felt cold. His face was haggard, and the mention of Mary Dee's name had made him look murderous.

"What's wrong? Whatever it is, you know Virginia will understand. She's smart, she's nice, and she really loves you."

Chuck nodded. "I know she'd finally understand but it'd hurt her so much. And she's not my only worry. I have another reason not to say anything."

"Good Lord. You can't keep something that bothers you this much all bottled up. You need to talk to someone. Your wife is the logical person."

"No, I can't talk to her. I've gone over and over the problem and I can't see a way out really. I do need to talk to someone. Maybe I could talk to you. You're clever and I trust you. Maybe you can see a solution for me. Although, I don't think there's a chance in hell that you'll understand this. You're from a whole different era."

I could feel my horrible curiosity rise up and fight with my sense of decency. I mean I really wanted to hear the reasons for his dilemma and his gigantic secret but I had to admit I probably wouldn't be much help to him. I don't have enough experience to be able to give him anything but my twenty-three-year-old outlook on love and semi-serious coupling. I was hardly a good marital counselor.

"Chuck, you know I'll keep your confidences to the grave, and I'll give you the best advice I've got, but it just isn't going to be that great. I don't know anything about marriage or even really serious lifetime relationships or sexual problems or well, anything very complicated. Got to be honest."

"I appreciate that. I could have guessed you aren't a burnt-out party girl with too many hard miles on you. But this isn't just a married couple sort of problem. It's my job too."

"Your job? I can't imagine your job being in question. But maybe I'm a little better qualified to talk to you about agency problems. And naturally I'm curious. So if you need to talk, I'll gladly listen. And I promise to keep anything you say to myself."

Chuck took a minute and then said, "Haven't you wondered why I've kept Mary Dee in my creative department?"

"Wondered? Are you kidding? It's always been the Number One topic of gossip in the creative department."

"And did you come up with any good reason why I hired and kept Mary Dee?"

"We guessed she had convinced you she was a terrific art director or a good mentor to the young artists or a creative genius. I thought maybe she was an old friend. I figured you had to have a good reason to keep her around. Her presence has been a glaring exception to your good taste."

"Friend? I hate her, Amy. I really hate her. She's like a killer drug that has been injected into the whole creative department, the whole agency. She's divisive, competitive, dishonest and a born trouble-maker."

I added, "And she's a stealing, lying monster. She hasn't had a new creative thought in her life. She keeps her job by claiming other people's ideas. She just stole a great campaign from Peter that he's been working on for months. Went right to Geno and told him it was hers. He believed her, and Peter's devastated."

"I know all about that, Amy, and don't worry. Peter will get the credit, the awards and the boost in salary."

"Hallelujah! None of us thought you realized what a piece of trash Mary Dee is. Let's get rid of her."

Chuck kept going, as though I hadn't spoken. "We have a creative department now that could and should be winning a lot of the big national advertising awards. I really believe that Mary Dee keeps everyone so riled up and at each other's throats that we never get our best work done."

"So fire her, fire her. We'd all back you up. Even if she ran to Geno Pirelli—whom I darkly suspect she has a naughty hold on—if the whole creative department was on your side—and they would be—he would have to listen."

Chuck rubbed a weary hand over his face and then said, "It isn't Geno I'm worried about. It's Mama Pirelli."

"Mama? She never gets involved with advertising."

"But Mama does consider our personal lives her business. If Mary Dee went to her, I'd be out on my ear without a recommendation or a bit of severance. To get the same kind of job, we'd have to leave Minneapolis and Virginia would hate that."

"So would I and everyone in creative."

"Thanks. Most of all, I'm proud of what we've built, and I can't stand to think of Mary Dee ruining all that work and effort."

I thought about it but I just couldn't imagine Chuck doing anything that would get him in that much trouble with Mama. I asked, "So what's Mary Dee know about you that Mama would care about? How much can she know about your personal business anyway? You never see her out of the office, do you?"

"She'd be the last person Virginia would invite to our home, that's for sure. But there's one thing you don't know, Amy."

"And that is?"

"Mary Dee was in my high school class. Class of 1966, the old West High School in Uptown Minneapolis."

A gleeful thrill shot through me. Mary Dee, carefully preserved Mary Dee, was over forty instead of the late twenties she claimed. And I knew this juicy delicious fact and I could spread this juicy delicious fact all over town. Whoops. I had promised not to tell. Promised on my word of honor. Oh, the waste, the waste.

"High school was a long time ago, Chuck. No one cares about the dumb things you did in your teens. Everyone is certifiably crazy then."

"This is hard to explain to anyone your age. It was different when I was in high school. I've loved Virginia since the first time I laid eyes on her in our freshman year. We started going steady as sophomores and were inseparable all though high school and college, except for a short break-up when we were seniors. We had a big fight, and I wouldn't give in. Neither would she. So my friends—some friends they were—said I should start dating someone else. Make Virginia jealous. So I did and it lasted two months."

"Surely she's forgiven you for that. That's not a big deal."

"Yes, it was. A big, big deal. The other girl and I got close. We didn't have anything in common but sex. But at eighteen, sex assumes major importance. Virginia might forgive me for that. But not for all the years I've lied. And if she left me, or if Mary Dee told Mama Pirelli, I'd be fired. Mama's big on that Choose Chastity Committee."

"Of course Virginia would forgive you. That happens to kids. Oh, Chuck, no . . . don't tell me that the other girl was Mary Dee?"

"Don't be absurd. Mary Dee was as big a witch in high school as she is now. Her basic nature was fully formed. No, it's not that."

"I don't understand. What's to forgive? Everyone screws around."

"Almost everyone, but not Virginia. She was and is a romantic. She wanted us to wait until we were older and really pledged to one another. She also wanted to be always, forever, eternally the only woman in the world I would ever have sex with."

"Wow, that's crazy. I mean wow, that's different."

"Of course, it was crazy. But I tried because I knew I wanted to spend the rest of my life with Virginia. Naturally, it got harder and harder, and we were both so frustrated that we started fighting. I think I could have gotten her to speed things up a bit, but instead I gave her an ultimatum. And she gave me the boot. "

"Chuck, I could have told you ultimatums don't work with smart women. That's not the end of the world either. Tell her now. Apologize. She'll understand."

"Yes, she would've if I'd told her then. But I was too young to even trust my own good sense. So I didn't tell her about it. And now it's too late. Mary Dee is into it. She knows I never told Virginia, and she's threatened to make things a lot worse."

I said, "Mary Dee knows, has always known?"

"Oh, yes. The girl was a friend of hers. When Mary Dee applied for a job, I knew her portfolio was weak and I had heard rumors about her. Her former boss told me plenty. The good ads she showed me I knew were probably borrowed from others."

"So why didn't you kick her flat little ass right out of there?"

"She reminded me of my two-month high school romance. She said, naturally as a member of my creative team, she'd be too loyal to ever mention it."

"Chuck, chill. This all happened years ago. If you'd lost your job, you could have gotten another one easily. You're really good and you have a great reputation."

"I know. Mama finding out would have been very inconvenient. The big problem, the reason I let Mary Dee stay and ruin the agency was my wife. I didn't want her to know."

"She's too smart to dump you for a short-lived romance that happened years ago."

"It's not the sex Virginia would mind. It's all these years of lies."

"Surely it can't still be that important."

"It would be devastating."

"But why?"

"Virginia thinks we have this unique, incredible love story and marriage, based on our single-minded passion for each other. It's the rock bottom of her belief in our marriage. It's also the basis for her trust in me. If she finds out I've been lying to her for years, she'd feel the marriage was a sham, that she couldn't trust me."

"I don't think so, Chuck. I think it would hurt. But not as much as all this secrecy hurts. She suspects there's something wrong, and you won't tell her what it is. I think that's what's eating at her. Tell her. Start over."

"Maybe I will. But I still have to worry about Mama Pirelli and getting fired."

"Go to Geno. Maybe he'll grow enough of a backbone to face up to his mother. I know he won't want to lose a talent like you on his account."

"I'll think about it. I can't go on like this. Telling maybe wouldn't hurt as bad as all this. I wish I had done it last week. Now maybe it's too late."

I felt something hot on the back of my neck. Joe had gotten back from the hospital. I turned to see him with Mary Dee, who was clinging to him like a spastic worm. He was standing closer to me than I'd thought and he looked serious. How long had he been standing there? Did he hear any of what Chuck had told me?

I'd been so involved with my conversation I hadn't noticed. Chuck had just confessed to his hatred of Mary Dee and a reason why he might like her out of the way. Permanently.

And I had promised not to tell anyone anything about what he had told me.

I had also promised Joe to keep my ears and eyes open. I had bragged that I knew I could help solve this case quickly. Now I was in the middle of another muddle of my own making. I couldn't tell and I couldn't not tell.

# CHAPTER ELEVEN

A QUICK RETREAT WAS CALLED FOR. I wanted to get away before Joe could ask me what confessions Chuck had been pouring into my ear. I also wanted to quit watching him being mauled by Mary Dee. If she got any closer to him, I'm sure he could charge her with sexual harassment. I started for the door and was stopped by Deputy Mike.

"Sorry, Amy. You'll need an escort if you're going to your room. That's orders from the big guy."

Before I could get my mouth open to deliver my opinion of the Big Guy, I felt strong fingers sort of massaging my shoulders and heard Joe's voice. "I'll take her up, Mike. I need to question her."

"Okay, Joe, but you better be careful. She's a handful, just like you said."

Joe was busy laughing and agreeing with Mike about what a character I was while I was seething again, an emotion I seemed to feel regularly around him.

As we started for the door, I said icily, "Well, you'll have to wait until we get upstairs to question me. I can't very well climb all over you here, the way Mary Dee did while you . . . ah . . . questioned her. I assume after watching the two of you, that's the usual way you interrogate women."

Joe didn't answer, just kept chuckling as we climbed the stairs. He opened the door to my room with a passkey, pushed me gently inside and kicked the door shut behind us. Then he backed me into the door and proceeded to kiss me. A lot of little firecrackers went off all over my body and I, well to be honest, I kissed him back. For a long, long time.

Finally I pushed him off me and said, "Police brutality!"

Joe started moving in again as he said, "You didn't seem to mind. That was you kissing me back, wasn't it? And responding like crazy, right?"

"That was simply a nervous reaction."

"Oh, Amy honey, if that was a just a nervous reaction, your nervous system must be shot. But let's not waste time arguing."

"You could have gotten in a lot of trouble you know. What if someone had come in while you were molesting me?"

"Oh, is that what you call it? You didn't have to worry. I locked the door."

"Well, what if I filed a complaint against you for your strange interrogation techniques?"

"I wasn't interrogating you. I was kissing you."

"Everyone would say you were abusing your powers. And I have proof. You left the proof all over me. Fingerprints with your DNA."

"True, but there are still lots of untouched areas. Please don't be upset, but they'll have to wait. First we'll solve this murder and then we'll talk about more fingerprints in more places. Be patient."

The ego of the man was so enormous I was literally tongue-tied. Then we looked at each other and both started to laugh. He was way too conceited, but he was damn funny and really good looking. I knew there might be more fingerprints if we didn't hurry up and solve the mystery. And really I didn't want any more. I was feeling guilty. I knew that Ryan not calling me for a week or not apologizing was no reason for me to fool around like this. And I was also pretty sure Joe was married, which made my behavior even lousier.

"Quit clowning around, Joe. If you really have questions for me, get on with it or go away."

"I have all sorts of questions for you, Amy. Let's start with the basics and then move on until we can get to all the things you know and are not willing to tell me."

I couldn't think of a smart answer for that. I did know things I wasn't ready to tell. I got up and moved to the other bed and got a little more composed before I answered him.

"Well," I said finally, "fire away. What do you want to know? I'll answer your questions if, for every one of my truthful answers, I get to ask you a question and you've got to be truthful."

"That's a deal. How old are you? You look about sixteen."

"I'm twenty-three. How old are you?"

"Thirty. Just turned."

"Are you married?"

"Hey, hey isn't it my turn to ask the next question?"

It was his turn but it annoyed me that he was going to wait to tell me his marital status. I could tell from the look on his face that he knew I was annoyed. So I tried to make my face an unreadable mask and told Joe to get on with his questions. We went through all the basic things—job, family, addresses past and present, home phone number—mine—he wouldn't give me his. Of course the hound was married. So when it was my turn I tried again.

"Is there a Mrs. Joe Bear?"

"Yes, there is. A really nice Mrs. Joe Bear. I think you two could be good friends. Would you like to meet her?"

My blood curdled, and I felt like pushing Joe out the door and locking it. How could he get it on with me when his nice wife was sitting home? She was probably taking care of their two, no three, tiny Bears. I could see their little faces, pressed against the window waiting for their philandering Papa to come home. Maybe I should push him right out the window.

"Amy," Joe said, "You should see your face. I was kidding you. There really is a Mrs. Joe Bear but she's my mom. And I bet you'll love her."

Better and better. Not only was he not married but he was already planning for me to meet Mother. Actually, I had no intention of getting serious about anyone but Ryan, so Joe's Mom was irrelevant. It's always an upper getting attention like this from a good-looking guy though. I don't have to act on it, do I?

We got back to the questions and it was getting harder and harder to keep all my secrets safe. I told Joe that there were good friends at the agency that I simply refused to consider as suspects or to talk about. My hands-off list included Angela, of course, Chuck and Virginia Pylon and Peter Andrews and his partner Mark Rollings. I told Joe right up front that there would be no chats with the law about my friends.

"That leaves us with plenty of other suspects and I've my suspicions about all of them," I said.

This made Joe happy, I could tell.

"Well," he said, "let's have it. Give me some of your darkest thoughts."

"Do you want them in descending or ascending order?"

"I don't know. What is that?"

"I could start with the person I think is the most likely to be a murderer and go down the list to the person I think is least likely. That's the descending option."

"I'm fascinated. Go on."

"Or I could start with the least likely to murder and go up to the ones I consider most vicious. In ascending order."

"Do it in any order your suspicious little heart dictates."

"Well, I could also do in the order of the suspects I dislike the most. That would be the most fun for me."

I could see that Joe was getting a little weary of my game. "Do it. Just do it, please."

'"Okay, okay. First, I think it could be Mama Pirelli. She's a strong-minded Sicilian from the old country. These people are used to handling their own problems. They don't go running to their lawyers to sue enemies. They just get rid of them. Mama couldn't do a murder herself but I'm willing to bet that she knows lots of guys who would do it for her for a price. So opportunity would be no problem for Mama. I'm a little hung up on her motives because I don't even know who her target might be. She seems to dislike everyone. I'd say Mary Dee is high on her list though because she's after Geno. But Mama could be gunning for anyone."

"Not your sweet old Italian Nonna then," Joe said.

"That's for sure. I've also given some thought to the other not-so-sweet old lady in our group. That's Harriet Smythe-Larson. She has a great motive. Her only son, Mac Larson, has also been fooling around with Mary Dee. This could ruin Mac's chances in conservative politics if it gets out. Mary Dee has a rather unsavory reputation."

Joe said, "Ah, the sadder but wiser girl. But not for me, of course. I like them young and inexperienced. Well, maybe not inexperienced but without the unsavory bits."

"How very classy of you. Well, Mrs. Smythe-Larson doesn't like me very much either. Mac has his roving eye fixed on me right now. She hates me because I'm not on anyone's social elite list but also because of my religion. So she has a sort of motive for the removal of two possible victims. But her opportunity for murder is really limited."

"Why? Can't she walk? She seems almost as fat as Mama."

"No one is as fat as Mama Pirelli. But Mac's mommy couldn't possibly climb a tree ladder carrying a heavy gun. And, clever old monkey that she is, I can't imagine where she could find a gun for hire. Her social circles seldom have members like that. But I'd like her to be guilty if that counts."

"The lawmen of Bayfield and Sawyer Counties will continue to suspect her then. And when we're through with crime, I'd like to hear a little more in depth about just how fixated Mac Larson is on you."

"There's no time to get into that right now. And there's no reason at all for you to ever get into the subject. Focus. We have a murder and an attempted murder to solve. Mac's crushes aren't important. But maybe he is, as a suspect. He has a really solid motive, lots of opportunity and an off-kilter conscience."

"I'm heartened to hear this. Doesn't sound like you share his romantic fixation or you wouldn't be offering him up to me as a possible murderer. Even the most callous of women shrink from turning their lovers in."

"I'm not Mac's lover, never have been, never will be. He's a now-and-then date, a step up from weekend television. If he tried to kill Mary Dee, well, it's tempting but wrong to condone it, and I don't really. If he's the one who hurt Angela, I want him caught and punished."

"So do I, Amy. Let's get down to business. Tell me what motive or motives Mac had for getting rid of Mary Dee."

"Mac has been having an affair with Mary Dee for the past two or three years. Everyone at the agency knows all about it. She sometimes talks about it as though it were a grand passion rather than the tawdry little affair we all thought it really was. She drops hints that he was urging her to become engaged, like he was really crazy about her. Mac, on the other hand, only talks about her to brag about their seamy sexual exploits to anyone who'd listen and wasn't actively nauseated."

"Sounds like a good motive," Joe said, "for her to kill him."

"I thought so too, until I found out yesterday how old she was. Mary Dee has already had all the plastic surgery her face can take and she's getting desperate."

"Meow. Pull in your claws and tell me about his motive for wanting to do away with the much improved Mary Dee."

I was getting way too distracted to think about someone else's motives. Joe had moved across to my bed as we talked. Then he moved closer and had taken to rubbing my shoulders and had now moved down my back. I squirmed away, and he moved in even closer and started nibbling on my ear. This had to stop. In a minute or two anyway.

I finally got up and moved across the room and sat down in front of the mirror at the dressing table. My cheeks looked flushed, my eyes dreamy and sort of out of focus.

I had to think of something to say, so I asked Joe if he had been taking notes.

"I've got everything so far. If you want to start sweet-talking me, I can always hit the pause button."

I decided not to dignify his remark. Instead I told him about Mac's motives.

"Recently Mac's starting talking about Mary Dee in a very respectful, friendly way. You know, acting as though they were good friends. This is really suspicious, as Mary Dee has no friends. Oh, she's had affairs and once in a while she'll gang up with someone to do something foul. But just be friends? Never. So when Mac started toadying up to her, it was odd. If he intended to kill her though, he might pretend to really like her first."

"The change in his attitude isn't really proof of guilt. Maybe he just changed his mind about her."

"Never! Of course that's not his only motive. Minnesota GOP leaders are starting to court Mac. He's always wanted to be in politics. Well, 'wanted' is the wrong word. Expected to be as a divine right is more like it. He sees himself as having been chosen by a Higher Power to rule the country. His mother thinks so too and has been pushing him since the day he was born. She has the influential friends, and she has the money to back him up. But Mary Dee could derail his train easily. She has a bad reputation and now that I know how ancient she is, I can see how she'd make Mac look really bad. The king makers would drop him in a flash."

"Okay. I can see that this could be a motive. But it seems rather skinny."

"Well, of course, Mary Dee is also blackmailing him. She knows how bad he wants to get into politics."

"Whoa, Amy. That's a pretty serious charge. Got any proof? This would really be a red hot motive for Mac."

"Actually not proof absolute, but she's such a snake I believe it might be true."

"Get the proof, and then we'll put him away. On second thought, don't *you* try. Exposing a blackmailer is dangerous."

"I'll be very careful. I'll come up with a foolproof plan."

"Leave it alone, Amy. As an old lawman up here used to say, a foolproof crime plan always has at least one fool in it who'll give it away. Let's get back to old Mac. What about opportunity? When the murder took place, Mac was in the middle of the Birkebeiner. Everyone left together and everyone swears he was with them."

"True, but all they actually know is that Mac started out with them. Once the race got going, it was every man for himself, and you don't really have time to notice where all your friends are. He could have slipped off to the side, let them go by, done the murder and then got back in the line and started skiing again."

"That's true. But awfully hard to prove."

"That's not all. Mac is a really good skier. He's awfully fast. Last year he finished the Birke in just a little under three hours. This year his time was almost four hours."

"That is a big difference. We can check the time, right down to the second, with the officials. We'll be meeting with all the judges and all of the helpers to see if anyone saw anything unusual. For example, someone who was seen getting back into the race and not at an aid station."

"The trail is over fifty kilometers, Joe. He could have gotten off anywhere."

"I know. We're going to completely recreate the race with local skiers who finished in each five-minute wave, if we can find them and they're willing to cooperate. Maybe one will remember something. Maybe we'll get lucky."

"Maybe I can tell Mac that I saw something on that old fire road. Then he'll have to eliminate me."

"Forget it, Amy. You stay out of it. We've had one murder and almost a second. I really don't want you to be number three before I've had my way with you."

"If your way with me includes my dumping ice on your conceited and overheated head, you're on. Otherwise, I wouldn't count on it, Joe. I don't like men who plan my life for me. I've had more than enough of that lately."

"Ahh, another hint as to what you've been up to before meeting me. Well, never mind. I don't have an unblemished past either."

Interpreting my glare correctly, he grinned and continued. "Back to Mac again. I'm surprised you think he might be capable of the planning that went into the two crimes. He seemed quite stupid to me."

"He's not really. It's just that he is so focused on himself that he has no idea of how he appears to others. It's emotional stupidity."

"Have you thought about his alibi for Angela's accident?"

"Yes and it doesn't hold up. Mac took an extra hour this year to finish the race. So he had plenty of time to stop and kill. Remember, Angela went out to ski the trail after the race was about half an hour underway. If she saw Mac somewhere on the trail alone and not where he should have been, she'd wonder what he was doing there. She could have blown his alibi for the murder. He would have had to try to kill her on the trail. When he failed, he would have tried again. He could have put Angela in that chair too. No one was keeping track of where anyone was the night Angela was hurt. Everyone was drinking and roaming around. He'd have had all the time he needed."

Joe was quiet for a moment and then shook his head and said, "It's not airtight yet, but you've made a damn good case for Mac."

"I've got some thoughts about other people too," I said. "That's the problem with this crime. We have too many people with good motives for killing Mary Dee. It's a crowded field because she's so nauseating. So far we have little hard evidence. But I think I have one really solid clue. Where was Mac during that extra hour on the trail? And what was he doing?"

# CHAPTER TWELVE

T HAT WAS THE LAST CLEAR THOUGHT I remember having. I almost fell asleep while Joe went on with his questions. I knew it was time for another nap. But Joe said we'd better get on with the questions.

We had just started talking things over again when the sound of Ojibwa drumming and chanting suddenly filled the air. I jumped nearly to the ceiling before I realized it was only Joe's cell phone. Those new, creative ringers drive me batty. But I'll bet Joe never missed a call. It was loud enough to wake the whole hotel. He spoke little but listened carefully to a rather long report. When he was done, he turned to me and told me that the call had been from St. Luke's Hospital in Duluth. Angela was waking up.

"I'll be going to Duluth in about ten minutes, and I'd like you to come with me. I have a feeling Angela'll be pretty scared when she wakes up and your cute little Irish face will be a welcome sight."

"I do not have an Irish face. I am fifty percent Irish and fifty percent Italian. What I have is a one hundred percent American face."

"Actually, Amy, I'm the only one in this room who is one hundred percent American. You're not even a half-breed."

"And you're not even . . . ahhh." I couldn't think of a thing to say that was awful enough to wipe that grin off Joe's face, so I just sputtered to a stop. Then I walked over to the door, opened it and made "get out" gestures to Joe.

"I'm leaving, my little Mick Minx. Be at the front door in ten minutes, please."

I'm sure they heard my door slamming all the way to the front desk. I wasn't sorry about that. I was just sorry I was a little too slow to hit Joe with the door.

As I was getting ready for the trip to Duluth, I was having severe guilt pangs. I was appalled at my behavior with the big, bad sheriff. What had I been doing making out like a teenager during a murder inquiry? It just wasn't like me. I wasn't cold but I wasn't easy either. So I was confused. Joe was great looking, but really I didn't know anything about him, his life or his relationships. I was hot for a gorgeous, funny stranger. My self-respect took a dive.

The guilt was pretty much all about Ryan. Yes, we had sort of broken up last week, but I knew it was temporary. He was the best part, the forever part of my life. Was I really ready to take chances and have him leave forever? I didn't think so.

There wasn't time to brood. After a shower, clean clothes, hair repair, and an instant coffee, I grabbed my purse and met Joe at the front door.

The ride north from Hayward to Duluth was one of the most beautiful in the country, I thought. We took Highway 27 straight north from Hayward to Lake Superior. For miles, we went through the enormous white and red pines of the Superior National Forest, past sparkling, deep blue lakes and those rocky, fast-running rivers of Wisconsin I loved so much. Turning west at the big lake, we came through Superior and out over the lake on the high Richard Bong Bridge. The St. Louis River was on the left side, Lake Superior on the right, with the steep hills of Duluth straight ahead. An awesome sight, one I never tired of.

The ride was pretty darn quiet until Joe spoke. "I want you to know that I've never acted during an interrogation like I did last night. I like you, Amy. You're smart and funny. I want to get to know you lots better. If I've offended you, I'm sorry.

I guess it's also pretty obvious I'm very attracted to you, but I'll try to behave professionally and keep my hands to myself."

"Well, it wasn't all your fault and actually it wasn't all that bad."

We looked at each other and smiled and a lot of my embarrassment was gone.

"Let's get back to the murder," I said. "Did they give you any idea of what condition Angela's in for questioning? I hope by this point she can tell us at least some of what she knows."

"She was just starting to wake up when my deputy called. I think she'll be a little confused and very tired. Let's go over the most important things we hope she can tell us. We'll talk fast and get some in before she gets too tired. I hope she can tell us if she saw anything before she got her head bashed in last night. The person who hit her is almost surely the murderer. So I think we should ask her that first."

I nodded, "I agree. If she has enough strength for another question, we really need to know who she saw on the trail that surprised her so much the morning of the race."

"You're right. That's the second important key, I think, to finding our number one suspect."

When we arrived at St. Luke's, we were taken directly to Angela's room but found it empty. Joe's deputy met us and explained that Angela had just been taken away for more tests or x-rays. He'd go down and bring her back to us when they were finished. Joe and I went into her room, sat down and waited.

I said, "You know I always thought that murder mysteries were fast paced. But there's a lot of waiting to this one."

"There are always times during an investigation when nothing seems to be happening. However, I can think of something we might do now to pass the time, if you're bored. No, no forget I said that. I am on my best and most professional behavior."

"Thank goodness."

"I hope you don't really mean that, Amy. Do you?"

I just laughed and didn't answer. This guy would flirt as he was being led to the firing squad for lascivious behavior.

There was a rumbling outside. I opened the door and looked down the hall. I could see what appeared to be a large pile of blankets on a gurney coming our way. Under the blankets, Angela was back, accompanied by one of her guards. She saw Joe first and fear filled her face. I spoke quickly, "I'm here Angela. And this is Sheriff Joe Bear. Don't be scared. He's actually not nearly as fierce as he looks."

The deputy laughed until he saw Joe's eyes on him and then he tried to turn the laugh into an extended cough. I could see that Angela had relaxed a bit but she didn't say anything. They put her back into the bed, and then two nurses got busy attaching what looked like a spaghetti junction of cords, drips and wires to Angela. When they were finished, one of the nurses left the room but the other one stayed, keeping a close eye on her patient. I moved my chair in close to the bed and took Angela's hand. She was so thin, her hand felt full of nothing but bones.

"Angela, Sheriff Bear was hoping you'd feel well enough to answer a few questions. Do you?"

Angela nodded her head and tried to say something. She whistled when she talked and her breath sounded as though it was coming through a kettle of thick syrup.

Joe said quickly, "We'll try to ask you things you can answer yes or no to. So don't strain yourself. If you have to use words, go slowly. We'll do our best to understand."

I said, "Angela, remember going out to your car during the big spaghetti dinner?"

Angela nodded.

"Do you remember who hurt you? Do you remember anything at all?"

A quick shake and then Angela stated to speak. "No, no . . . tunk."

The only word I recognized was "tunk" and I guessed she meant trunk so I asked her if she was looking for something inside the trunk when she got hit and she nodded again.

Obviously, there was nothing more to be gotten with questions about her accident. So we switched to what she had seen the morning of the race that had worried her.

Joe went first, "Angela, do you remember deciding to go for a ski on the trail after all the racers had gone?"

Angela nodded.

"Do you remember meeting someone on the trail, maybe even talking to him or her?"

Angela looked confused and a little scared. She finally shook her head.

I said quickly, "Maybe you didn't actually meet anyone. Maybe you just *saw* someone. Please tell us, Angela. We'll keep you safe."

"Am safe." Her answer was garbled but understandable.

"I'm glad you're not worried about being safe. I'll bet the person you saw didn't see you. Good. But you're worried about something."

There was a quick nod of agreement from Angela.

"Are you worried because you saw someone you know well? Do you think he or she saw you? Someone you work with? Are you afraid you'll get that person in trouble?"

Now Angela indicated yes and then no. She had seen someone but she didn't believe he or she had seen her. And it was someone she knew but didn't care about.

I got positive signs on the next questions I asked. "Was it someone you work with?" A nod. "Was it a man?" Nod. "Okay, was it a friend?" Shake. "Someone who works for Pirelli Pasta?"

Angela shook her head to this question. I had been so sure it was Mac she had seen that I was stunned. Then I remembered that Mac did all the Pirelli legal work but that he was actually self-employed. She still could be talking, or nodding rather, about Mac.

"Does this person work for Pirelli's in some way but office somewhere else?" That's a yes. "Are you talking about Mac Larson?"

Angela made a "who knows" shrug with her arms and shoulders so big that I was afraid she'd dislodge the bandage that covered a good part of her head. So maybe it was Mac or maybe not and perhaps he wasn't the one she meant now. Next she made writing movements as though she were holding a pad and pen.

"She wants to write something. Don't you, Angela? Yes. She's nodding yes."

Joe quickly pulled out a pad and pencil and handed them to Angela. Her hands were shaking so much she could hardly hold the pencil. After a real struggle on her part, she showed me the paper. It had nothing on it but a great, big V. And Angela was all done writing. The pen had slipped out of her hand and fallen to the floor. Her eyes were closed and she looked pale.

The nurse bustled up to her, pushing me out of the way and started doing something magical, I hoped. She said, "You'll have to leave now. If she wakes up after a while and seems strong enough and able to continue with this, I'll come and get you."

Joe was frustrated but didn't say anything until we got out in the hall. "What do you think she meant by that, Amy? You know her friends and family. Can you make a stab at it?"

"I know her family and the friends that she has now. But before we really got to know each other, she had lots of other friends who don't come around any more. And she had a huge book full of clients, business contacts, and every good photographer in town. They all wanted her then and they've all disappeared now."

Joe said, "I think it must be someone she still sees. Seems more logical because otherwise why would she have thought that you would know whom she meant? Think. Who is the mysterious V?"

"The only V I can even think of in my life, let alone hers, is Victor, the little dog on the old RCA records. My grandma had hundreds of them."

"Funny, although not really helpful. Is there a V you can think of at the agency or at Pirelli's? Let's see. I think I have that list of the people you came up to Hayward with right here. Take a look."

We put our heads together over the list but there was no one from either Pirelli's or the agency group that had a first name that began with a V except Virginia, and she was off limits and had an alibi.

Joe was stymied. "No one in your group has a name that begins with a V. Maybe she isn't thinking clearly. Or maybe it's a nickname?"

"You mean like Prince Valiant or Vixen? Nope. Can't be anything like that with us clever types. Anyway if we were the kind of people to make up cute nicknames, Angela would have known it."

"So we're agreed that V didn't come up to Hayward and isn't staying at Telemark with you. How about the agency or Pirelli people who didn't make the trip?"

"God, Joe that's hundreds. Pirelli Pasta is a big place and our agency has nearly a hundred people."

"Think about it. It wouldn't have to include Pirellis. Angela doesn't work there."

"But she goes there all the time doing scut work for Mary Dee. Things like picking up product for shoots."

"Well, let's go over the agency people, Amy. We have some time before Angela wakes up and we might as well use it. So think."

"Okay, okay. I'll go floor by floor and imagine I'm looking in the offices as I go by, and perhaps I'll be able to remember most of the names. Or I could try and read the little removable nameplates. Or should I use another method like my ascending and descending lists of possible suspects who were not on the list of my fellow travelers?"

"Don't care how, babe, just do it. And what do you mean removable nameplates?"

"Advertising isn't the most stable of professions, Joe. So they never nail nameplates to the wall. They slide in and out of a groove and are easy to remove, just like we are. So if you're just interested in my sweet little salary, you should know you won't be able to count on it. One bad campaign, and I'm outta there."

Joe laughed but I could see by his face that the names better start coming fast. I started with the creative department and went mentally over every member of Chuck Pylon's teams of writers and artists. No V's.

Then I walked my mind down the hall and went through all he offices for print production, graphics, television production, traffic, public relations, and creative services. Nothing. Didn't anyone name his or her babies something that started with a V? Where were all the Vernons and Velmas, Virgils and Vanessas?

Switching my mind to the next floor up, I went by media, accounting, personnel, account executives and I ended at the door of our leader, CEO and President Hy Voss.

"Voss!" I screamed. "She saw Voss, our president and CEO. I think he's the only V we have. How stupid I've been, Joe. I was just thinking of first names. The name of the agency is Pylon and Voss for heaven's sake."

"We were too hung up on the list you gave me the other night. We needed to broaden our search, and that's just what we've done. Tell me about Voss."

"He can't be the one she saw. He's just not the type. He's a nice enough guy for a suit but he's very formal and a real city dude. He's the kind of guy you can't imagine without a tie, the kid who never played in the snow. He's no sports addict. His one physical attribute is how well he holds his liquor. He's a sales meeting legend for that."

"Heavy drinkers have occasionally been known to do dumb things, Amy."

"No need for childish sarcasm. I didn't think about Hy because I knew he wasn't originally slated to be up in Hayward for the Birkebeiner and because I know his type. It can't be him."

"Convince me."

"He's so not the criminal type. I'm telling you, Hy just couldn't be our guy."

"Too sweet a guy? Even Genghis Khan loved his mother."

"No, not that. He's anything but sweet. Hy's too careful, too conservative. And he's so smooth. I can't believe he'd ever get in so much trouble that he'd have to kill to get out of it."

"A sad fact is that conservative, middle-aged men do go chasing hot, young babes, which does end in barrels of trouble. He also might have gotten involved with Mary Dee."

"Impossible. Hy doesn't have the time."

"Wretched sinners that we are, men have a reputation for making time for romantic trysts."

"He is the most scheduled human being in the world. He has a wife who probably knows where he is every minute of every day. He's taken to and from the agency in a limo and he has to be home on time. They have an extremely busy social life."

Joe shook his head sadly. "The poor devil."

"You got it. They go to every gala, opening, and ball given for one charity or another in both Minneapolis and St. Paul."

"Now I want him to be the guilty one even though you tell me he doesn't have the time. I hate those society bums who get to take huge tax deductions for eating big, rich dinners. Mom can't get tax deductions for her proven Ojibwa medicines that she makes and gives sick people."

"Forget it, Joe. Our tax laws favor the wealthy. You can never shake the money out of really rich people without giving them a great meal first. Hy Voss gets plenty of them. And all that socializing with the swells is another reason he can't be our man. Hy's very well known around town. He always has his picture in some society page or magazine. He'd be spotted anywhere, especially with a trashy blonde like Mary Dee."

"Okay, I'll have to agree with you. Hy's life is an open book. He no doubt lusts after women only in his heart. He has no vices, no secrets, no sinful hobbies."

"Hobbies! Oh, my gosh, I'd forgotten Hy's big hobby. He loves guns. He's also known to be a crack shot. Someone told me that Hy could shoot a whisker off a mouse."

# CHAPTER THIRTEEN

W E HAD RUN OUT OF QUESTIONS, but we had to wait until Angela woke up again. We hoped she'd confirm that Hy Voss was the man she had seen on the trail. During the long wait, Joe and I spent the time making notes on the absolute evidence we had to date. It was a short list. The suspicious list was a lot longer and often only the product of my creative imagination. It was serious business, but Joe and I still managed to crack each other up with regularity.

When Angela woke, the nurse called us to come back. Once inside Angela's room, I asked, "Was it Hy Voss you saw, Angela?"

She nodded and went right back to sleep. The nurse assured me that sleep was the very best medicine for her now and that I could quit worrying. That made me feel a lot better but I hated to leave her alone in Duluth. Joe said we had to get back to Hayward.

"I wouldn't mind staying here overnight with you, Amy. However, I think I might have a tough time being elected next fall if I let our sex life interfere with business."

"You are delusional. We don't have a sex life now and the chances of the two of us ever having one is just a figment of your overheated libido."

Joe just laughed. He acted as if he thought my peevishness was adorable. We waited for the elevator in the lobby. When it arrived, the doors opened and out came a Duluth policeman and with him Angela's grandparents. They fell on me and started asking me questions in Czech. Their old faces looked sick with worry.

I hugged them both and smiled as wide as I could and kept saying, "Angela okay. Angela good." Then I turned to the deputy and asked him where the interpreter was.

"Didn't figure we'd need one," he said. "I'd heard that Ms. Krajak was awake."

"We do need one," Joe said. "Angela isn't able to talk. Get an interpreter pronto or we'll scare these two old folks into hysterics or heart attacks."

As the deputy hurried off to find an interpreter, I went into my best mime routine. Grinning like a demented clown, I put my head down on my hands and feigned sleep, complete with little snores. The Krajak's looked more scared than ever. Luckily, the nursing supervisor came over at that point and said firmly, "Angela is fine. She's sleeping. It's nine now, you can see her at ten o'clock." She pointed to the clock behind the nurses' station as she talked and her no nonsense attitude seemed to reassure the Krajaks. They settled down to wait as we left.

As we came out of the hospital, people were yelling, and blinding lights shone on our faces. I instinctively put my elbow up to cover my face with my arm before I heard Joe say softly, "Don't worry Amy, it's only the media."

Only the media? It was a zoo. There seemed to be hundreds of them all shouting at once and vying for the best shots. I could see the logos for all three of Duluth's television stations and a host of radio call letters on other microphones.

I felt like crying. My fifteen minutes of fame and how did I look? Like I had just climbed out of a dumpster. Why hadn't I combed my hair before we came out of the hospital? Slathered on some lipstick, eye shadow, and mascara? Had a good night's sleep last night so I wouldn't have bags under my eyes? And changed my yesteday's wrinkled and passé clothes for an outfit with a little style. If she was watching television, my mother was going to kill me.

One yelled, "Can you tell us the name of the woman in the lift, Joe?"

Another wanted to know if Joe had caught the killer yet. Then I heard one yell out, "Is that the killer, Joe? What's her name?"

Oh no. Not only did I look like a bag lady but a murderous one at that. When I put my arm up to shield myself from the bright TV lights, they must have thought I was trying to cover my guilty face. This was the last straw, I thought, but I was wrong. Joe proceeded to make it ten times worse. First, he gave the press my name, which dashed my hopes of not being recognized, even by my mother. And then he went on and finished me off.

Joe said, "No, we don't know who the killer is yet but we're closing in fast. I'm not giving out the name of the woman in the lift yet. This is Amy Connolly. She is a friend of the woman in the lift. She's nobody important to our investigation."

Nobody? He was calling me nobody? Not important? He'd better have a damn good excuse for saying that. I stepped off the stairs of the hospital, roughly pushed myself through the media and headed for the sheriff's car.

The air inside the squad car was even frostier than the outside but Joe didn't seem to notice. He was on the radio being patched through to someone who did matter, I suppose, Deputy Inga Johnson. He was telling her to find Hy Voss and to find him fast.

"I'm pretty sure he's still in Cable or Hayward. He lives in the Twin Cities and is an owner of Pylon and Voss. Call his home or ask the people from his agency if they know where he's staying in this area. If that doesn't work, put out an APB on his car and start calling all our four-star hotels and inns. When you find him, I want you to hold him for questioning until I get there. Ask him politely to wait for me. He's the type who'll lawyer up fast if you give him a reason. If there's one thing I don't need right now its some smart-mouthed, big briefcase, fat-fee, city lawyer getting involved."

When Joe was done giving orders, he started the squad car and headed back towards Cable. Then he turned to me and said, "What are you thinking about so quietly? Not like you. Got any new ideas?"

"A nobody doesn't get ideas and when she does you wouldn't want to hear about them. They wouldn't be important."

"Is that what's got your busy little tongue silenced? I certainly didn't want to give our murderer an idea that you were involved or knew anything about the crimes. Unless you'd like the thrill of being hunted down next. I said that for your protection. We were lucky no one noticed you were the skier by the body yesterday."

I could see that he was right but I wasn't about to thaw out yet. I said haughtily, "And thank you for letting me know how you feel about lawyers. One of my brothers is a lawyer and so is a longtime gentleman friend of mine."

"Before you ride off the wrong way on that high horse of yours, I should tell you that I got my J.D. at Yale six years ago. So I don't hate lawyers. I'm prepared to love your brother."

I started to laugh. "I know you'll like him. He's a smart-mouthed, big city, fat-fee lawyer but he spends ten percent of his time on no-fee cases that interest him."

"And who's the gentleman lawyer friend?"

"This is your business, because? Let's move on. I have a scary new thought. If Hy didn't see Angela he'd have no reason to go after her. So it has got to be someone else who feels danger from Angela and might make a second attempt on her life. And we don't have a clue who it is."

"I've thought about that too. Have you told me about everyone who could have a motive for all this? Another agency or Pirelli Pasta person who was up here for the race?"

"There's quite a few more," I said. "The ones I won't discuss with you are Angela, Peter Andrews, his partner Mark Rollins and Chuck and Virginia Pylon."

"There's the V you could be looking for."

"No! It is not Virginia. She's an even worse skier than I am. The others I haven't mentioned though are all possible suspects."

"So who's left?"

"There's Geno Pirelli and his wife Lucia Antonucci Pirelli. Geno is the heir apparent to Pirelli's Pasta, the only son of Mama Pirelli, the founder. He is the head of the company now in name only as Mama runs things. I can't imagine Geno as a murderer, frankly. He lives to have a good time, is a heavy-duty womanizer and spends most of his time avoiding and trying not to get caught by his spooky wife."

"What makes Lucia so spooky? And why doesn't Geno like her?"

"Well, she wasn't his choice and I mean that literally. Mama went to Italy and chose Lucia for Geno, brought her back, and they were married six months later. Geno seemed to go along with the deal but he was really getting even with Mama without ever saying a cross word to her."

"And how was he doing that?"

"No bambinos. Mama needs bambinos to carry on the Pirelli line. That's what Mama wants. And she's not getting it."

"Neither is Lucia from the sound of it. How does she like being ignored?"

"At this point I would say that Lucia hates everyone in America. She goes around wrapped in black with a curdled expression, darting positively evil eyes at everyone. She's sneaky. I've seen her listening at doors and to telephone conversations although she says nothing and pretends not to speak English. But she must. I think her aim is to catch Geno with another woman, get an annulment and a lot of money and get back to Sicily."

"Sounds like a plot line from the Godfather. Lucia would definitely have a reason to kill Geno and maybe Mama or both. Unless you're wrong about her and she's really crazy about Geno and has started trying to rub out the competition. That might be Mary Dee, right?"

"I don't think so. Geno is charming, great looking and rich. I can't see him with road kill like Mary Dee," I said.

"I suppose she could have gotten something dirty on him and threatened to tell Mama or Lucia."

"That would be more like it. He's spoiled, used to getting his own way. And Mary Dee isn't smart enough not to get caught. But he's too lazy to murder anyone."

"Lucia must be an unlikely candidate. She's small and slight. She might have climbed that tree but with a heavy gun?"

"I agree. She'd never have been out in the middle of the race with a gun. For one thing, she hates winter. Also, I've never seen her exercising hard enough to raise a sweat. But it doesn't leave her out of the running. Not really. Just like Mama, Lucia would know people from the old country who could help her out with the shooting."

"Get out of that Pirelli and agency business, Amy, please. I've never heard of a crowd with more possible murderers and more possible victims. You're not safe."

"Don't be silly. Everyone likes me."

"I'm glad your experience with the rabid media types in Duluth has left you with your usual healthy ego. But that agency sounds like a murderous place. I hope your list of suspects is at an end."

"Not quite. There's the chauffeur, Stephano. He works for Mama, supposedly just to drive her hither and yon in her big limousine. But he's always sneaking around. I caught him listening at our door while I was talking to Angela. Gee, that was just yesterday. So much has happened, I feel like I've been up here for weeks."

Joe said, "So we add Stephano to our list as a possible hit man without a known motive himself. Anything else you're not telling me?"

"There's plenty I'm not telling you but nothing about the murder. Speaking of people not talking about things, what's all this law degree from Yale stuff? Why were you keeping that hidden?"

"Just hadn't come up. And I knew you weren't the kind of woman who'd like a guy just because he went to a big-name school. I could tell you were more the type to go for a strong sexy guy."

"I am. Do you have a friend like that you could fix me up with?"

"Way cruel, babe."

"Sorry. Why aren't you practicing law?"

"I do that one day a week on the Rez. I'm a tribal judge. I prefer that kind of law to the corporate boardroom stuff. I've had a part-time job with the tribal police from the time I was eighteen, so the sheriff thing was a somewhat easy jump."

"Okay, but why? I can tell you're good at the job but it still isn't practicing law."

"You're wrong. It's a lot of law, the hands on kind. I'm a lot better sheriff because I understand the law, and are careful of people's rights. I love the job, and it was a blast running for office."

"Ah, now we're getting to a kernel of truth. You're planning on politics as your career."

"It already is my career. I've been elected to my job twice. Now I'm planning to run for the Wisconsin legislature next election. Where do I want to go from there? I'd like to be in a position to really change things in this country. And that means Washington, D.C. There's a whole lot of unfairness and stupidity going on there."

"I agree and I'm impressed. I'll campaign for you. You seem honest but time will tell," I said, yawning a bit.

"I am and I'll hold you to that promise. Now, why don't you take a nap? You've been up a long time."

I agreed with that. So I laid back and let the night rush by. The huge pines that had been so beautiful in the sun now were like great, dark shadows pressing in on either side of the car. It was a cold night and the moon kept going under little wispy black clouds. Anyone could be out in those woods. I didn't think I could sleep.

The next thing I knew, I heard someone screaming. I tried to open my eyes, but there was something huge and black in the way. It was Joe, bending over me.

"Amy, wake up. You're having a nightmare. We're back at Telemark and you're okay. I'm afraid you've had too many scares in the last couple days. You need sleep. C'mon, let's get in where it's light and warm."

I looked at my watch. It was after midnight, but the Chippewa Room was still full of Pirelli and advertising people. They gathered around me, anxious to hear about Angela's health. I hoped the anxiety was for her recovery and not because one of them was worried about what she was saying.

"Turns out she didn't know anything about the murder," I lied. "She was just scared. I can't imagine and neither could she why someone tried to hurt her. She didn't see a thing, can't imagine who it might be."

Again, a collective sigh. Was it happiness or relief? I didn't care which as long as it kept Angela out of a devil's eye. There were more questions, but I was asleep on my feet. I had to get to bed before I fell to the floor. Joe came up and took my arm.

"Let's get you to bed, Ms. Connolly. I'll walk you to your room."

We got to my door and Joe opened it and nudged me in ahead of him. The room was dark, and Joe was closing in on me when I saw a dark form rising from my bed. I screamed so loud I'm sure I roused the whole floor. I could hear the curious opening doors up and down the hall. Joe pushed me behind him, got his gun out and snapped on the light. Ryan Kelly, my long-time boyfriend, sat up sleepily and then got up fast when he saw me and Joe, who was pointing the gun at him.

"God, Ryan, you scared me. What are you doing here?"

"I read about the murder in the paper this morning. I came up to take you home."

"Well, son," Joe said. "You have no right to be here, and I want to know how you got into this room. You didn't have to worry. Amy has been well taken care of."

Ryan stiffened when he heard the insulting, diminutive "son" and gave Joe a glare that was just short of lethal. "I have every right to be here. And it's obvious you haven't been doing a good job guarding Amy, if that's what you call it. The room was wide open when I got here and had been searched. And, officer, I'm not your son."

The room reeked of testosterone so I acted fast to avoid more trouble. "You can both help me look around to see if something's missing. I'm a tad casual, so I don't really think it looks like anyone was pawing through my stuff. This is kinda how I left things."

I looked around but didn't find anything missing. And I had probably just forgotten to lock the door. Ryan and Joe both spent their time folding clothes and putting them in drawers or hanging things in the closet. Two neatniks. How lucky can a messy girl get?

When we were done, I said, "Ryan, I'm dead on my feet but I do want to talk to you. So sit down a minute. Joe, you can question Ryan in five minutes. I need some space right now. Okay?"

Joe nodded agreement. "Five minutes. I'll be waiting for you outside and we can take it from there. Have a good sleep, Amy."

As soon as the door closed, Ryan said "Who's that old geezer and why is he so familiar with you? What have you been up to?"

"That old geezer is just a few years older than you are and it's none of your business. You gave up that right when you stormed out of my apartment two weeks ago. And you haven't called since."

"I was giving you time to cool down and consider my very handsome offer of marriage. Actually, I was waiting for you to cave in and call me."

He laughed and walked over to me and hugged me tight. I looked up at the face I'd been in love with ever since I could remember. Blond curly hair, bright steady blue eyes and a smile, ready to break into a grin. He looked wonderful, he felt wonderful, and he smelled wonderful. Oh, dear lord, I really was in trouble

# CHAPTER FOURTEEN

I LOOKED IN THE MIRROR AFTER RYAN LEFT, and I thought I could see TRAMP written on my forehead. I was really exhausted though so it probably was just an optical illusion. But how could I have the hots for two men at once?

Well, no sense in dwelling on my behavior. I really hadn't done anything so terrible. I promised myself I'd flirt no more and got ready for bed. Ryan and I had agreed to meet early for breakfast. It was now 2:00 a.m. Monday morning and I needed my sleep.

Joe called three minutes later to say he was letting most of the Pirelli Pasta and agency people go the next morning. Most would be heading back to the Twin Cities but he'd asked four to stay for more questioning. Hy Voss had been found living in grand style at Lakewoods Resort. Joe requested his presence for questioning at 9:00 a.m. and asked me to be there too.

"I can stay," I said. "But my friend has to return to the Cities. So I'll need a ride."

"As soon as I figure out which suspect is the least likely to be the murderer, I'll get you a ride back to the Cities with him. I'm coming down but not until Wednesday. That is if we don't get a confession before that."

I was a little mad at the cavalier way Joe seemed to be handing me off and said so. "Well, what if you're wrong? You could be sending me off to my death."

"No, I'm sure you'll be fine. It'd be better if you could wait until Wednesday. Stay with me, and I'll drive you down."

That sounded like a plan that could get me in more trouble than I could handle. I agreed to stay just until late afternoon Tuesday. I knew that even staying another hour here was not going to be a popular decision with Ryan. But I was in on the hunt and I just didn't want to stop. I avoided thinking about how big a part Joe played in my decision to stay. Like Scarlett, I'd think about that tomorrow, after I'd had a good sleep.

The next morning Ryan and I had just settled in the Prince Hokum Room for breakfast when Joe and a deputy came in. Joe sat where he could look right at me and did. Luckily, he was too far away to overhear us. Ryan had me square in his blue, blue eyes as he started in on his list of questions for me that I didn't want to answer. I felt like a pingpong ball between two giant cats.

"A lot has happened to me in the past two weeks, and I've wanted to tell you about it," Ryan said. "I'm sorry I haven't called. I've been out of town a lot. Way out of town, actually. I have to be in court this afternoon so I have to get back. Are you packed? We can talk on the way."

Things got a little frosty when I told him I was going to have to stay a few more hours but he mellowed out when I promised I'd be home tomorrow, hopefully, by dinner. He convinced me that I should walk him back to his room after breakfast to help him pack. Instead, I just sat on the bed and watched him. I loved watching Ryan work. He packed like he did everything, quickly, gracefully, without a wasted motion. He was a super athlete in almost every sport and I'd always liked watching him move. While he packed, we talked in that wonderful shorthand way people did with someone they loved and trusted and who loved and basically trusted you. We went over the days since our fight and caught up completely except for one thing.

Proving his intelligence and his sure knowledge of me, Ryan never mentioned the Joe thing. It was as though he didn't think it was worth talking about. If he'd made a big deal of it, I would've had to rebel and we would have brewed up a whole new fight.

Growing up with three older brothers, I'd had all the bossing I needed or wanted by the time I was six years old. Ryan knew how much I hate being told what to do. So instead of quarreling, we laughed and kissed, and it was sweet and exciting and dearly familiar. We loved one another. It was that simple.

After we finished packing, I went downstairs with him. I was saying goodbye to Ryan in the lobby when I saw Joe talking to one of his deputies by the desk. So did Ryan. He grabbed and kissed me, bending me down almost to the floor, like we were in a romantic movie. When he let me go, he was laughing and I had to laugh too. Ryan was staking out his territory with a capital R. I pushed him away and pointed him towards the door before my reputation was completely shredded.

Too late. Mrs. Smythe-Larson was standing right behind me and as I turned she said, quite loudly, "Whore."

"You're mistaken, Mrs. Smythe-Larson. I never ask payment for my sexual favors. So 'whore' is really an inappropriate word."

I left her, mouth open and sputtering, face purple. I walked towards the desk and Joe, who was laughing. I had hoped to find him seething with jealousy, but no. He was laughing. And he was gorgeous. My stomach did that little quivery thing it did when something super sexy comes my way. Maybe Mrs. Smythe-Larson was right about me.

Joe said, "Amy, congratulations. Most people here started the day a little more slowly. They had some coffee, read the paper, and maybe said a quick goodbye to departing friends. But you've had two dramatic scenes in the last two minutes."

"Not my idea. I never plan to make scenes. They just seem to happen to me."

"Sorry. I was sure you were enjoying yourself. Let's get our times down for today. Most of the Pirelli and the Pylon and Voss people are checking out and getting ready to leave. We'll finish things here and then start the questioning of Voss, Larson, Dee, and Pirelli. I need you to help me, and we'll get it done in a few hours. Okay?"

"Okay," I said doubtfully, because it certainly sounded like more than a day's work to me. "We'll be through by early afternoon, I hope."

"Should be. If we don't wrap up the case today with a confession from one of the three, which I doubt, I'll be down in the Twin Cities on Wednesday. Then I'll do more in-depth interviews and cross-checking with the others. Tomorrow, we're having a small recreation of the race. Would you like to stay and play victim?"

"That sure sounds like a super offer. Let me think. This would mean another long day on skis, lying in the snow, and getting frozen and shot?"

"Don't be dramatic, Amy. No one will be shooting at you."

"Gosh, Joe that part was tops on my list of your fun plans. I hate to turn any of them down, but if I don't get back to the Cities, I might get fired."

The lobby was crowded now with people carrying bags and skis, going home. Those staying were talking with the receptionist about late checkout times. Others were passengers who had lost their rides because of drivers being kept for questioning. Most of them were taking things in stride, just quietly milling about, looking for rides home.

Not Mrs. Smythe-Larson, of course. She grabbed Joe from behind and was screaming about multiple lawsuits.

"You will pay, Sheriff, I can promise you that. You will pay for my inconvenience. You will pay for daring to involve My Boy in all your sordid murder business. And you will pay for his loss of reputation. Free him and send him home at once if you do not want to feel the full force of my anger."

As she was bellowing at the top of her voice, Joe didn't look too worried. He probably figured she was already operating at gale force. He was patting her shoulder and easing her towards the door as they talked. When they ran into Mama Pirelli, the noise from Mrs. Smith-Larson came to a full stop.

"Mrs. Pirelli, I can't tell you how glad I am to see you. I'm hoping I can get a ride back to the Cities with you. This man has had the audacity to ask my son to stay and help him with this murder."

"My Geno stay too. So what? I go now. You can come too but not if you talk loud. I don't like loud."

The look on Mrs. Smythe-Larson's face was a study in the passing moods of fury and pragmatism. She needed the ride and she certainly wouldn't want to spoil little Mac's legal retainer with Pirelli Pasta. So pragmatism won.

While the two women collected their luggage and arranged for bellhops to take the bags outside, Lucia Antonucci Pirelli came in and stood talking to Mama. She spoke in Italian but I gathered that she needed a ride home too as Geno had been asked to stay.

I knew the Pirelli women didn't like each other. Put the two of them in one car for a two-hour or more ride, then stir in the awful Smythe-Larson. That ride was shaping up to be hotter than a Sicilian wedding.

In the background of the hubbub in the lobby of Telemark, I could hear beeping, the steady honking of a dozen or more cars. The sound kept getting louder and louder. As Mama Pirelli and her riders made for the door, I decided to go outside too to see what was going on. Plus, there was always a chance Mrs. Smythe-Larson would blow up again before she left. I did love to watch those ill-tempered scenes she was so good at providing.

Outside, it was a madhouse. There were way too many cars in the turn-around circle in front of the hotel with skis and baggage piled everywhere and people trying to squeeze between cars to claim their bags. One car had the hood up and several men were attempting to push it to one side.

Most of the cars were packed and ready to go with steamed up drivers at the wheels. That accounted for the constant, ill-tempered honking. It was hysterically funny. A real traffic jam in Bayfield, probably the least populated county in Wisconsin. There was a huge, almost empty parking lot a few feet away from the front doors of Telemark. Instead, everyone must have decided to pull up right in front of the hotel to load up and save time. Then they were caught.

Mama Pirelli's limo was the stopper in the sink of progress. Her big car was parked crossways in the driveway blocking everything behind it. Added to the confusion, the bellhops had simply left their luggage in the road next to the car. It was still snowing, of course. It was a giant mess.

Mama and her guests came out of the hotel and went down and stood by the car. They paid no attention to the noise or to each other. They looked around for help and when none came, they opened the limousine's doors themselves and got in. I could see the heads of all three of them, all in black, looking like three giant crows.

They were looking straight ahead, just waiting for some serf to come and wait on them. They weren't talking so they hadn't gotten into any quarrels yet.

I heard a car door open and my name called. It was Peter Andrews with his partner, Mark Rollings. They both looked mad. I fought my way past a lot of angry people, climbed over their luggage, hunkered down by Peter's little Mini Cooper and looked in. Peter was in the driver's seat, his long legs right up under the wheel. Why do short men drive big cars and tall men small sporty jobs? Interesting question for a psychiatrist, don't you think?

I leaned my head into the open door and said, "Hi, guys. You don't look too happy. I'm sure Sheriff Bear will get this mess sorted out quickly and you'll be on your way home. So cheer up."

Peter said, "You wouldn't be too cheery either if you'd been waiting almost an hour for Mary Dee."

Mark joined in, "We're never happy to be with Mary Dee let alone wait for her. You'd think when she had the nerve to bum a ride with us, after all the dirt she's done to Peter, that she'd at least be on time. That was one hour ago. I have to get to work. It's my shift this noon and we're short-handed."

Mark was part owner and chef at a new restaurant in Minneapolis, La Grande Tavola. He'd been struggling to get it going and this weekend was his first vacation in months. He'd missed another full day of work yesterday. His business partner, the other chef, had already worked all weekend so Mark could get away. He would probably not be amused by another long shift today.

"So why does Mary Dee need a ride?" I asked. "How did she get up here? On her broom?"

"With Mac," Peter said. "Isn't that a scream? He invited her and then his horrible mother decided to come along too. It was very last minute so he couldn't find another ride for either of them. That must have been a hell of a trip for Mac."

At that moment, Mary Dee came out of the hotel and posed at the top of the stairs. She was wearing her skin-tight racing suit and carrying her skis. She was tall and thin and the outfit suited her, I had to admit. She waited a minute until she thought everyone had seen and admired her and then slowly, slowly oozed her way down to the car.

She gave a little wave and smile to Peter and Mark who paid no attention to her. Then she turned to me. "Ah, you're still alive, Amy. I had hoped that whoever shot at you Saturday would have finished you off by now."

"It's terribly kind of you to worry about me Mary Dee. I'm just fine. I'll be staying on awhile and then I'll probably ride home with Mac."

"I suppose he'll have to take you with him although I'm sure he won't want to."

"Au contraire. Mac asked me to drive up to the Birkebeiner with him about one second after the trip was announced. I was already planning on going with Angela so I had to decline. That made room for his second choice. Oh, that was you, wasn't it?"

The gloves were off now, and Mary Dee's good mood and manners evaporated. She snarled at Peter. "Get out of the damn car and put my skis in. And be careful with them. They probably cost more than your monthly salary."

"You've already given me two pairs of your skis to bring home." Peter said. "The rack on the roof is full. I'll have to put these skis in the car. And they're all wet. They're going to ruin my upholstery."

Our jolly little get-together of co-workers was interrupted by the arrival of a truly enormous Cadillac SUV. It swept into the circle, taking the very last spot.

The circle now was completely blocked. If Mama Pirelli didn't get her limousine going pretty soon, there was going to be massive road rage.

Out of the car stepped Hy Voss, looking annoyed. He paid no attention to the fact that he had blocked traffic. He didn't speak to anyone but hurried up the steps and into the hotel. His frozen-faced wife stayed in the car. She was probably afraid she might catch something common from us.

The horns got even louder. Joe came out of Telemark with two of his deputies. Now the cars would get moving. He went over to Mama's car and opened the door. I sidled up close so I could overhear.

"Mrs. Pirelli, you've got to get your car out of here. It's holding up traffic."

"Don't tell me. Tell Stephano."

"Your chauffeur. Well, where is Stephano?"

"He not here. He must be here. But he not. You find him."

"I'll look for him, Mrs. Pirelli, but first we need to get you moving. Have you got keys for the car? Yes, you do. I see them in the ignition. Your man must have left the car here and gone off on some errand. So we'll look for a another driver to move your car out of the driveway."

Joe sent one of his deputies down the line of cars, looking for someone to drive the limo with the three crows out of everyone's way. He came back, almost dragging a very reluctant Mark Rollings. Mark got in and started the car and was pulling out when a squawk came from the back seat. It was Mrs. Smythe-Larson in excellent voice.

"You can't drive away and leave our baggage in the street. I have some very expensive things in my bags. If they're stolen, you will pay for them."

Mark turned off the motor and got out of the car. An absolute cacophony of car horns and some very loud swearing followed. Mark and one of the deputies collected all the women's bags and brought them to the back of the car and tried to open the trunk. There wasn't a trunk key on the key ring. He knocked on the door and asked Mama., "Where's the key to the trunk?'

"Find Stephano. He got key."

Joe came back to see what the problem was. "I'll go up and look for him, Mark. He's probably still in his room. Try and stay calm, kid."

It seemed like he was gone forever but it probably was only about five minutes. When he got back, he said, "Well, I didn't find Stephano, but I did find another key ring in his room. One of these should open that trunk. Let's get those bags in and get these ladies out of here."

Joe, the deputy and Mark each picked up a bag and started for the trunk. I thought I might as well help. So I grabbed a bag too and followed them. They found the key and got the trunk open. Then they just stood there.

"My God," the deputy said. "What the hell is that?"

"Looks like a body," Joe said.

I pushed in to get a better look and was very sorry I had. It was Stephano. His eyes were open and he had thrown up in the bag that covered his head and was taped tight around his neck. I've never seen anyone who looked so dead.

The cars all suddenly quit their honking and things got very quiet. Some people were getting out of their cars and coming closer to get a better look. Joe reached in a put his fingers on Stephano's neck. He shook his head. Obviously there was no pulse.

The limo doors opened and the three women got out. Mama just stood there looking evil as always. Mrs. Smythe-Larson was screaming something. Lucia came around the car, got to the trunk and looked in.

"Oh *non, non.* Papa, Papa, *si prega di parlare con me. Se sei morto* Papa?"

She whirled and looked at the crowd slowly coming towards her. Then she screamed, low and dark, an inhuman scream. "*Assassino, assassino!*

# Chapter Fifteen

THE HORNS HAD STOPPED. There was no sound except for the car motors and an echo of the scream. The air was breathless, cloudy and ominous. I was so scared I must have quit breathing. I felt as though I might faint.

And then it got worse. Lucia Pirelli bent into the trunk of the car and started scrabbling at the plastic bag, trying to get it off so she could touch her father's face. And all the while she kept screaming. When she got the plastic off, she reached in and tried to clean off his poor, grotesque face. Finally, she just picked Stephano up against her, like a doll, a dead doll. It was horrible, horrible.

Then in counterpoint, another roaring noise began. It was coming from behind us, violent, foreign and terrifying. I turned to look and saw Mama Pirelli stomping down the length of her long car, coming on in full throat. I didn't understand her but I heard the anger, knew that Mama was in a terrible place. She marched slowly towards Lucia and the dead Stephano loudly screaming what I guessed were vile thoughts, murderous threats in Italian.

It took her what seemed like hours to reach her daughter-in-law and her former chauffeur. When she did, she planted her feet firmly on the ground, leaned on her cane and closed in on Lucia, who didn't even seem to know that she was there. Mama then gave her such a slap across her face that Lucia's whole body slammed backwards, almost knocking her over. Adding insult to injury, Stephano was knocked out of his daughter's arms and into the dirty snow of the driveway. Lucia quit screaming. Quiet descended.

"Just what the doctor ordered," one of the deputies said to Mama. "She was obviously in shock. You did the right thing, lady. I know you did it to be kind."

Mama turned her dark and dreadful eye on the deputy who wilted faster than the foam on a cheap latte. I was close enough to see Mama and there was no kindness to be seen on her nearly purple face. She looked like murder. She was angry. She was telling Lucia off and telling her why.

Mama had good reasons to be so furious. She had been fooled by this girl and by Stephano, her father. They had kept this big secret, their father-daughter relationship, from the Pirellis.

Far from being her trusted lieutenant, Stephano had tricked and lied to Mama. And the daughter-in-law that Mama had so carefully arranged for her precious Geno? She was the daughter of a chauffeur, not the carefully raised princess, the beautifully schooled daughter of Italian nobility that Pirellis had been promised.

Stephano must have paid a real noble family in Sicily to pretend Lucia was their daughter when Mama came shopping for a bride for Geno.

"*Male!*" Mama suddenly screamed. "*Brutta prostituta.*"

Lucia suddenly came alive again and an ugly stereo conversation in snarling, liquid Italian filled the air. Mama, of course, was attempting to reduce Lucia to a blob that she could scrape up and send back to Sicily. Her face had gone from purple to puce. I would have been terrified. I was terrified.

But Lucia Antonucci Pirelli was made of far stronger stuff and was not so easily intimidated. She put her face close to Mama's and began a low hissing sound, freezing cold and evil. What from the lowest regions of hell, I wondered, was she threatening to do to Mama?

She kept getting closer and closer to the old woman and finally reached over and grabbed Mama's cane with one hand

and then pushed her with the other. Mama went down like a sack of mozzarella.

Unfortunately, Mama landed right on top of Stephano's dead body. Her face turned a color I'd never seen in my life. She somehow got to her feet and started kicking the body as hard as she could, which enraged Lucia ever more. She pushed Mama down again, and put her stiletto heel right smack dab in the middle of Mama's amazing stomach. Then she leaned down and began hacking up phlegm and spitting on her fat, old victim.

All of us onlookers were so amazed, and, truth be told, so entertained, by this better-than-any-movie fight that we just stood and gaped. Our civilized instincts should have kicked in and forced us to try to stop the fight but it was just too gripping. We knew we'd never see anything like it again.

And naturally we were all very, very afraid of the two women. Talk about tough. I wouldn't have lasted two seconds in a fight with either one let alone both.

Two of Joe's courageous deputies finally got between the two women and the horrible body. The first one got Mama under her two ham-sized arms and pulled her back and away.

Then he said in his comfortable, favorite uncle sort of voice, "There, there, ma'am, you just calm your old self down. You don't want to pop a blood vessel in your brain, do you?"

Mama snarled something back at him. She was so angry I thought the deputy was probably right. Her temper tantrum just might kill her.

"I'm sorry, ma'am," the deputy said. "I can't understand what you're trying to tell me. Could you try it in English? I'd like to be able to understand you."

Count your blessings, fellow, I thought. You don't know how lucky you are that you don't understand Mama. She probably just put a five-hundred-year-long curse on you, your children, your grandchildren, and all of your farm animals.

The other deputy was attempting to stay out of the way of Lucia's incredible reservoir of spit while he tried to stop her in her attempt to pick up her father again. She would lift the body a few feet off the filthy snow, and then when the body flopped about, she would lose her footing and down they'd both go. It was stomach churning.

The deputies managed to keep the two women far apart, and things were somewhat quiet. Mama was being walked back towards her car. Someone had thrown a car robe over what was left of Stephano. Lucia was sitting by the body, giving it little pats and talking to Stephano softly. It was heartbreaking. Where was that devil Geno? Why hadn't he come out of the hotel to help his wife and/or his mother? Talk about selfish.

Joe, his deputies and the guards from Telemark had managed to bring a modicum of calm to the whole scene. They had sent the rubber-neckers, who were not involved, back into the hotel. They had also gotten all the Pirelli people and the Pylon and Voss staff back in their respective cars.

I loved watching Joe directing the whole big mess. He was in full alpha-male control, and he looked powerful. He had managed to get people not used to taking orders, to do just what he wanted them to. He was making them march to his directions with no talking back, no threats of calling their lawyers. He looked calm, and he looked sexier than ever to me.

I remember reading once that a man having and using power was a strong aphrodisiac for a woman. Scientists claim it has something to do with choosing a good mate for procreation purposes. You know, one with lots of strong sperm. And one who could kill a dinosaur and drag the dead body home to feed the family. Now, why was I thinking about that?

Soon the cars were full of their original drivers and passengers. The idea was to take them one car at a time back into the hotel making sure no one was alone and able to slip away. Joe went from car to car, checking names off. This included everyone on the hotel register list of people from our group who had signed out that morning.

I decided it was time for me to get up and help Joe. After all, he probably could use my blend of creativity and common sense to figure out this latest murder. I mean, after you have all the facts in a crime, it's those little creative leaps that can actually solve things for you. Thinking outside the box. Using your god-given imagination to put yourself in the shoes of both the victim and the murderer. This kind of original thinking often resulted in fingering the right suspect. At least it always did in most of the murder mysteries I read. So I knew I was needed.

I started pushing my way towards Joe but was soon pushed back by a burly Telemark guard. He asked me if I had checked out that morning. When I said no, he took me by the arm and escorted me towards the hotel door.

I yelled to Joe and he finally turned and looked our way. He waved the guard on and ignored me. Well, I thought, he can just muddle around getting nowhere with all these murders. I had better things to do than help him anyway. I would just sit down quietly and start making my own lists of clues and suspects.

I could begin questioning people all by myself. Who needed Joe? I certainly was not going to share my ideas with him, the stuck-up, power-happy moron.

Suddenly I could hear sirens. They sounded like they were coming from every direction just like before. It was deja deadly vu.

# CHAPTER SIXTEEN

THE BURLY GUARD WITH THE GESTAPO-LIKE grip on my arm was deaf and dumb to my obvious charms and my attempts to get him to loosen his hold.

"Sir," I said, "I'm going to need to stop at the desk and get the key to my room."

"No keys."

"Well, you're going to have to get the hotel key then and take me up to my room so I can get my cell phone."

"No phones."

"I can see your point, but I do have a need to communicate. Please stop by the desk so I can send a fax."

"No faxing."

"I suppose getting a cup of coffee or a bite to eat is against the rules in Northern Wisconsin."

Finally he smiled. "Just for possible suspects. We starve them."

Funny man? I didn't think so. I wasn't smiling.

"Look," I said, "if you're planning on keeping me without food and phones for very long, you're going to have to arrest me."

Snickering, he said, "Joe said that could be arranged if we need to."

I finally shut up before he called the totally loathsome Joe, a person I had no desire to see. The deputy deposited me back at the Chippewa Room, our lock-up all day yesterday. It was torture being there in that windowless room when I knew exciting things were happening outside. Clues that only I might spot. A shifty, guilty look on someone's face that only I might notice. I had to break out.

I cheered myself up by listing all the ways I might humiliate Joe when I did escape. The perfect insult. The icy snub. Anyhow, there was no breaking out to be had. My troglodyte escort had settled by the door, and he kept both eyes on me.

I was the first one in the room, but the others started straggling in, one carload of people at a time. There were no smiles, no happy greetings from anyone. They all looked either grim or mad and some of them looked scared, too.

Telemark catering came to the rescue. With their legendary hospitality they arrived, bearing just-out-of-the-oven rolls and muffins, platters of fruit and fresh, hot coffee. Obviously, they had their standards to keep up. They would serve even murder suspects with aplomb. Being waited on always cheered me up, and eating sent my spirits soaring. Other people were comforted too. They started to chat together quietly. As the shock wore off, voices got louder.

Conversation came to a halt when Mama Pirelli came into the room. She clumped her way over to the largest and most comfortable chair and sat down. No one was getting up to go to her side, like they usually did. Even the most confirmed sycophants were staying away. No, I spoke too soon. Leaping across the room came Mary Dee, calling out loudly, "Mama Pirelli, you poor dear. I'm here to help. What can I do for you? Please, just name it."

Mama looked up, and the room went silent, waiting for her reply. "You go away. Go away now."

Mary Dee wasn't about to take that as the last word. She asked, "Mama can't I get you something? No? How about something warm to cover your legs? A nice hot cup of coffee? Just name it, Mama. I do so want to help you."

All this phony sweet talk was bringing on my gag response. Thank goodness for Mama. She removed Mary Dee's hand off her arm with a smart little rap of her cane. Then she got up and walked over and sat down next to me. I was pleased for a nano-second. Unfortunately, I was now close enough to smell everything Mama had been rolling around in out in that driveway. My gag response was now a reality. I didn't care if I got fired. I got up and moved away.

Practically our whole group was now in the room except for Lucia. She hadn't appeared, and I didn't expect her too. No one wanted a reunion of the two Pirelli women.

The Big Egomaniac, formerly known as Joe Bear, entered the room and got the crowd's attention. He was very serious as he spoke to us. "Ladies and gentlemen, again we ask for your patience and your help. Obviously, there's someone in this group with murderous impulses. We're going to find that person or persons as quickly as we can. We ask for your cooperation. If you have knowledge of Stephano's movements during any time yesterday afternoon, evening, or this morning, please let us know. If you have any information that you think might be important, please share it with us. You can talk to me or to any of the deputies

Your comments will be absolutely confidential. For your own safety, do not confide in other members of your group."

There was a long, indrawn breath from everyone in the room. People had their eyes on the floor or closed. I think they were terrified of looking at the wrong person, maybe a murderer or of looking guilty themselves.

Joe continued, "Don't put yourself in jeopardy by sharing information with each other. Telling the wrong person about suspicions you might have could get you killed. We'll be taking you out for questioning one at a time. It'll take some time, so please be patient. Before the questioning, you'll be taken to a room and searched. We realize this will be unpleasant, but I'm afraid it is necessary."

A growling noise, louder than a barn full of hornets, broke out. No one liked the search idea. Some even yelled that they be damned if they were going to be searched.

Joe put up a hand and silenced the room, "If you do not wish to be questioned without your lawyer being present, which is your right, or object to a search, let me know. We'll arrange a transfer for you to Sheriff's Headquarters in Hayward. You'll be detained alone in a holding cell until your legal advisor arrives and allows us to go on with the questioning. As we will be very busy here during the next hours, possibly all day, it may be a long wait for you in Hayward. We'll be as fast as possible, but we're very short-staffed because of these murders."

That shut everyone up as Joe had intended. They were all smart enough to know they weren't going to like a long wait in a holding cell. And they were too self-protective to object to being searched. That would be like an admission of guilt. Their objections were probably just something they wanted to hide, like an X-rated book or DVD, and porno pictures off the web they didn't want seen.

Joe continued, "Okay. We'll take you in order now. First you'll be searched and then taken in for questioning. When I announce your name, please follow the guard to another room. Ms. Connolly, please."

As I got up and walked over to the deputy, Joe said, "Thank you, Ms. Connolly. There'll be a female deputy there to help you. If each of you does this as fast and efficiently as possible, we can get you all released quickly."

Naturally, I ignored him completely. I was taken to another of the Telemark suites where a very unpleasant surprise awaited. Deputy Inga Johnson was to search me. She looked as uptight and unfriendly as always, and she also looked Spic-and-Span clean. I did not. She took one look at me and her lip went up in a sneer as she closed her eyes. Next she put on a cover over her uniform and then tight, rubber gloves on her hands.

She didn't bother with politeness. "What kind of landfill have you been sloshing through? You smell terrible."

"Listen, Princess, I'd smell a lot better if you'd allowed me to go to my room to clean up and brush my teeth. Now you'll just have to breathe and bear it."

"We couldn't allow you to be off on your own. You might destroy evidence."

"If I were you, Deputy Inga, I'd quit the social chatter and get on with the search. I'm feeling mighty like throwing up again. Must be someone's cheap perfume."

The search was so complete that I had to count old Inga as a person who knew me really, really well when it was over. She was plenty rough too and did unnecessary things like search through my hair backwards to really mess it up. Finally done, she delivered me to another room where Joe, a stenographer with a machine like a court reporter, and a guard busy with a tape recorder were waiting for me.

"Amy," Joe said, "everything you can give us about this latest murder or about anything actually, will be held in confidence. If it isn't of importance to our investigation, it won't be used. And our sources will be kept private unless they are needed in court."

"You're finally asking for my help?"

"Of course. I'm counting on you."

"Well," I said frostily, "I have noticed a lack of cooperation on the part of the sheriff's department in this county. There are citizens, like me, eager to help but some lawmen seem too bone-headed to let them."

Joe's lips twitched, but he didn't laugh at me. "I couldn't show you partiality out there this morning. It just wouldn't have been professional. But you know I need your input. You're smart and you're nosy. I mean curious. You notice more than most people, and you're quick-witted enough to put the right interpretations on what you've seen and heard. So tell me. What did you notice?"

A little mollified, I decided to quit the kvetching and help. I could deal with the "nosy" crack later. I sat and thought for a minute and tried to remember the things I had wanted to tell Joe this morning.

Finally I said, "It wasn't so much the things I noticed as they happened. It was more the things that I don't remember because they were NOT happening. First. Geno Pirelli. He was absent completely. Why didn't Geno appear? He must have heard all the noise out in front. His mother and wife were in trouble. Where was he? Where is he now?

"Second, Mary Dee. Peter Andrews and his partner, Mark Rollings, waited over an hour for her to show up as she had conned them into giving her a ride home with them. She was the last of our group to show up. And she was wearing her racing suit. Usually she dresses to the hilt. Why was she late. Why didn't she have time to change, and where had she been?

"Third. Mac Larson. I haven't seen him anywhere today, haven't seen him since early last night. It's very strange he wasn't there this morning to kiss his horrible mommy goodbye. She expects that kind of fawning from him. But this morning she didn't seem to mind. Why wasn't Mrs. Smythe-Larson upset?

"Fourth. Hy Voss got here at the last minute this morning. He was all dressed up, but I noticed he had those big, furry boots on. That doesn't sound important, but it's strange. Doesn't go with his buttoned-up personality. Not like him to be off in his dress style. Why the furry boots?

"Fifth. I haven't seen Stephano at all. He was not around yesterday afternoon, evening, or this morning. But Telemark should have a record of when he ate last. Our meals are included, but we have to sign for them. Stephano wasn't the type to miss a free meal."

Joe pushed back his chair and grinned at me. "I've got to say, Amy, you're worth all the trouble. I knew you were looking and, better than that, thinking. Have you got answers to any of your questions for me?"

"Not yet. I have just suspicions and vague ideas. I'll need you and your crew to do some digging for me."

I got up and walked to the door, turned and said, "While you're checking up on these things, I'm going up to take a shower and change my clothes."

"I'll escort you to your room to make sure you're safe. I have the master key."

Joe Bear with a key to my room while I took a shower? Didn't sound safe to me.

# CHAPTER SEVENTEEN

Nothing ever turns out like my imagining. Rather than being slowly and deliciously romanced by Joe Bear, I was dumped. After opening the door, he told me to hurry up and get changed, as he wanted me back downstairs as quickly as possible. He was going to set up a room where I could watch the questioning on closed-circuit television. Then he gave me a friendly little pat and pushed me through the doorway, shut the door and left.

I should be too proud to admit it, but I was disappointed. Of course, this was ridiculous. We were in the midst of a deadly investigation and a true crime hunter would have had her mind on finding the killer. Also, as I belatedly reminded myself, I was just about engaged to Ryan Kelly. Joe Bear had been a momentary twinge in my well-ordered romantic life. Yes, he was drop-dead good-looking, quick witted and funny. These are all things I liked to consider, not only essential but my due. But Joe was trouble I didn't need. Obviously I would have pushed him away if he'd tried something, as I was deeply in love with Ryan Kelly. Telling yourself lies and being able to totally believe them was one of the advantages of the creative mind.

I showered and made myself as irresistible as possible in fourteen minutes and went downstairs. Deputy Mike greeted me and escorted me to a small side room behind the main interrogation room. As I entered, I could hear Mary Dee's bossy, grating voice telling some lie or other.

Then Joe spoke. "Why didn't you have your bib and entrant number?"

"None of it was my fault," Mary Dee screeched. "I gave strict instructions to my go-fer Angela to be at my side when I started the race so I could hand her my jacket. Instead she sent her little dwarf friend to do her job."

"What's the dwarf's name?"

"Amy Connolly. I was busy getting my skis and goggles on. I told Amy to get my bib out of my parka and slip it over my cross-country jacket. She didn't do it and, in the heat of the moment, I forgot it. The bib was in my jacket so I went off without it. I think she probably hid it on purpose. She's a devious, nasty little dwarf."

Mary Dee is a consummate liar. Everyone who worked with her had always known that. These new lies were so brazen they took my breath away. How could I disprove them? The two of us had been alone when Mary Dee took off. I would just have to trust that Joe was a good enough officer to spot a liar like her. And he didn't disappoint me.

"Did anyone witness this exchange?" Joe said.

"No. That's not necessary. You just need to know what Amy is like and how much she hates me. She's terribly jealous. She knows I'm much more creative than she is and I make scads more money, too. And naturally, as you can see, I'm a lot better looking. It all adds up to her trying to get me thrown out of the race for spite. This is true. I know it."

True? I thought. She wouldn't know true if she was sitting on the scales of justice.

Joe asked, "When did you discover your bib was missing?"

"Oh, not until I had finished the race. What a shame. I had my best time ever. I was really flying."

"That's strange, Ms. Frank. The officials had no record of you finishing the race."

"Well, why would they? There were thousands of skiers out there to watch. I discovered the loss of the bib quite early, but I decided to ski on. I knew I wouldn't get a medal without it, but I ski for the pure love of the sport. When I had just about finished the race, I skied over to the side so I didn't go through the final checkpoint. That's why the officials missed seeing me."

Joe persisted. "We have a record of everyone coming in on video tape, and we could find no record, no sighting of you arriving at or near the last checkpoint. Or indeed anywhere at any checkpoint all along the trail."

"That certainly isn't my fault or my problem. They must have missed me. It's typical country-people inefficiency. I've been saying for years that they should take the Birkebeiner away from the hicks and move it down to the Twin Cities."

"Where they could run it right down Nicollet Avenue, I presume?"

Deputy Mike and I hooted with laughter in what I hoped was our little soundproof room. Mary Dee had nothing more to say.

"Let's move on, Ms. Frank. Can you tell me what you were doing and where you were late in the afternoon Saturday? Say between the hours of five and six-thirty. Also, do you remember anyone else with you or anyone who might remember seeing you during this time?"

"I was at the Pirelli Pasta party. Ask the dwarf. She saw me."

I had seen Mary Dee just long enough to fight with her, and I suddenly remembered that she was still in her racing suit then. After we were parted, I couldn't remember ever seeing her again. I'll bet no one had. She could have been outside looking for Angela.

"No one else we've interviewed so far has mentioned seeing you during these hours," Joe said.

"Oh, they were all a little drunk, I suppose. Ad people, you know, tend to drink."

"My deputies have not mentioned anyone appearing to be intoxicated when we spoke with your group after we found Ms. Krajak."

"They probably didn't notice. Your deputies' IQs don't appear to be the highest."

Joe said, "I doubt that you're an expert in IQ's, Ms. Frank. Let's move on now to this morning. We were told you were the last person to arrive where the cars were waiting outside Telemark. You were still wearing your racing suit, and it appeared to be covered with snow. Can you tell me why you were so late?"

"I suppose you heard that from that miserable little creep Peter Andrews. Well, you can tell him from me that his career is in the toilet. I'm going to fire him as soon as I get back to town."

"You aren't worried that such an action will make you appear even guiltier than you already do?"

A strange silence settled over the interrogation room. For perhaps the first time in her scheming existence, Mary Dee was at a loss for even one more little fat lie.

Joe said softly, "Nothing more to add? We'll have your statement typed up. We want you to read it carefully and sign it. We'll let you know when it's ready."

"Then I can go back to Minneapolis?"

Joe didn't answer and Mary Dee slinked out.

Dear, dear . . . it looked like Mary Dee was on her way to the Big House. I had a breathless dream of her dressed in prison orange. So bad with bleached-blond hair. She might be made a sex slave if any of the women could possibly be that hard up. No one could be. So in order to survive, she would have to turn to being a snitch. She was so dumb she'd get caught by Big Bertha and rubbed out. Poor, poor Mary Dee. My daydream continued until I heard Joe welcoming Mama Pirelli. I quickly made some notes on the Mary Dee interview as Joe asked Mama the standard questions.

As he got into the more sensitive questions, it quickly became apparent that Mama Pirelli was a whole lot smarter than Mary Dee. She wasn't about to give the law any ammunition.

Joe said, "Where were you from 8:00 a.m. until noon on Saturday morning?"

"I sleep. I am old. I need much sleep."

"Did you talk to anyone that morning from eight to noon?"

"No."

"Did you see anything out of the ordinary or see anyone during those times? Especially anyone who would remember seeing you?"

"You say I have strange men in my bedroom? You a nasty boy."

"I'll take that as a 'no.' Let's talk about Saturday night before and during the Pirelli Party."

"I am at party all the time. I am hostess. I say hello to everyone. Ask everyone."

Joe stopped to read some notes and then continued. "The catering manager states that he looked for you for almost an hour between 6:00 and 7:00 p.m. and that you were nowhere to be found."

"I was in the toilet. He look in toilet?"

"You state that you were in the toilet for an hour?"

"None of your business, nasty boy, but I tell you anyway. I have trouble with bowels. They take me much time. I am old lady. Sometime they don't work. Sometime too much. You want me to tell more about bowels?"

"No, let's talk about something else."

The questions went on for nearly half an hour more as the session wound down. I thought that if I had to call it, it would be Joe zero and Mama twenty-five. When it got to Stephano, Mama gave a little more information. She had a motive for wanting Stephano dead but quickly tried to explain it.

"No, I no kill Stephano. If I know what trick he play on me, I have him talked to. But I don't know until today. So I don't kill Stephano."

"You had no idea before this morning that Stephano was Lucia's father, your daughter-in-law's, father?"

"If I know, they both be gone."

"Gone? You mean you would have killed them?"

Mama laughed, "No. I just send them back to Sicily. Maybe not too healthy for them there."

No matter how Joe came at the Stephano murder, Mama managed to sound like she was telling the truth while giving Joe not an ounce of help.

My respect for Mama grew but, God almighty, she was a scary old lady. I decided there and then to get Chuck to take me off the Pirelli account. I'd rather take my chances with the board of directors of Murders, Inc.

She could be guilty of the first murder. It was a very long shot until you remembered that Mama was the 1956 Olympic Games Silver Medal winner in Cross-Country Skiing. A great skier like that might still pull it off if she needed to.

The attempted murder of Angela and murder of Stephano were a little more problematic for Mama to have done. She couldn't have put Stephano in the car trunk or Angela into that ski lift chair. Unless she had help. Stephano could have helped with Angela but who would have helped her with him? Her son, Geno? He's too careful, too self-protective. He didn't like Stephano but he liked his Mama even less. Mama would have to look farther away for help. If she'd hired a Mafia pro, Joe would never prove it because they rarely break their silence oaths. Mama left and the phone in my room buzzed. It was Joe.

"We're going to take a little break now. I'll send you in a sandwich and coffee. Then you'll have some time to get your notes down before we call in the next witness."

I said, "And where will you be dining, Sheriff Bear?"

"Thought we'd try the new seafood buffet at Lakewoods. I hear it's great."

"I love that buffet."

"Sorry, you don't have time to join us. I did want to thank you for your help but besides the time it would take, someone might see you with us at the restaurant and put two and two together. That would be dangerous. I can't allow you to take chances."

"I'll take my chances," I said. "I'm really, really hungry."

"If the others knew that you were giving information to the police, it would end your usefulness to us. No, it will have to be the sandwich for you today."

They could probably hear the gnashing of my teeth ten miles away. I said, "You're too, too kind, Sheriff."

# Chapter Eighteen

I SPENT THE NEXT HOUR AND A HALF alternately fuming and ravenously hungry, then getting excited about the possibility of Mary Dee being behind all the murders. Oh, I really wanted it to be her. And the more I listened to her testimony on the videotape, the more I thought it really could be. She told several lies that seemed to prove her guilt, to me anyway. She claimed she'd told me that her bib was in the pocket of her jacket and to be sure to get it out and give it to her. Not true, the big liar.

What Mary Dee actually said was, "Peter and Angela were supposed to be at the starting point with my bib. Better start looking for them, Dwarf."

This was her favorite, nasty name for me. She had equally insulting ones for nearly everyone who couldn't get her fired.

What I had actually said was something like, "Why should I? I don't work for you. I don't have to do you any favors, and I don't intend to."

I hoped that Mary Dee would be disqualified but she struck back.

"I need that bib number. So get it to me or I'll fire both Angela and Peter as soon as I get back to the lodge."

"Impossible. I'm a terrible skier. If I get in the middle of the Birkebeiner, I might get killed."

Mary Dee smiled her skinny-lip meanest smile and said, "That would be so wonderful I wouldn't mind not getting my bib number in time. Your decision, Dwarf. Go skiing and get hurt or get your friends fired."

I can still see her sneering face as she pushed off when her wave of skiers started. Mary Dee, a very good skier, looked like she was flying as she whizzed by.

Now she had told so many lies about me that I might be a suspect. I just hoped Joe Bear would believe my version of what went on that morning. I had Angela and Peter to back me up, of course.

What I still didn't understand was what reason Mary Dee had to lie about the bib. The only thing that made sense was that it gave her an excuse not to finish the race. She was a great skier. She could have finished with a really good time. So where did she go? It was just possible that she had been up a tree with a gun as I went by. I wouldn't have been hard for her to find me. She just had to spot a short woman, skiing badly and wearing her number. But where did she get the gun? Could I find out somehow if she had bought a rifle? And how did she carry it ? When did she hide it?

The big question of the day, however, was why would Mary Dee want to kill me? Sure, I did insult her, make fun of her and get people to laugh at her occasionally. All right then, I did my very best to get everyone to laugh at her all the time. But murder as a response to some bad jokes was a bit strong. I quit worrying about her reasons and just put down all my thoughts on her testimony and went on to watch Mama Pirelli's videotape.

I didn't get much out of her testimony. Mama was way too smart for that. She was a cunning, clever old thing. In spite of the overwhelming evilness that hung around her like a spooky miasma off a fetid swamp, I kind of liked Mama. She'd come to this country as poor as dirt and managed to build a food empire while caring for her very weak and dumb husband and her good-looking-but-do-as-little-as-possible son. I really doubted that, if Mama Pirelli had anything to do with either murder, she had left a single fingerprint on it. And if she'd had someone else do the dirty deed for her, it'd be someone who'd die rather than finger Mama or her Sicilian relatives and friends.

The door opened and Deputy Mike came in, burping a little and carrying a too-small sandwich. And to add insult to the tiny sandwich injury, he had no dessert for me. I gave him the notes I'd made on the first two interviews. He turned on the television monitor, and I could see Joe Bear getting ready to question Hy Voss.

Hy was a very good-looking man, silver-haired and always tan. He was pretty old, almost fifty I'd guess. His good looks were somewhat ruined by his constant sneering and supercilious expression. He was married to a member of an old-society Minneapolis family of bankers. Katherine Walker chose Hy Voss in spite of the fact that he was employed in the very déclassé business of advertising.

Her family, I'd heard, had never forgiven her in spite of the fact that Hy's agency was coining money and making Katherine even richer. She was seldom seen around our offices. She looked so patrician that I had always joked she probably had someone to pee for her.

Joe got all the preliminary data out of the way, and then started the questions with a real shocker, to me anyway. "Mr. Voss, during our search of your person and belongings, we found a rifle in your car. Our ballistic tests showed that it had been recently fired."

Voss responded without a shred of nervousness, "I know that. I found that my gun was missing early this morning. I had brought it up north with me to do a little target practice in my father-in-law's woods near Cable. He has a little two-hundred-acre spread there. When I went to pack up the gun this morning, it was gone. I immediately reported the theft to the authorities. You can check on that easily."

"We did check it out. So how did the gun end up back in your car?"

"It didn't. Someone turned it in to the desk at Lakewood this morning. They'd found it on the resort road. Lakewood noticed my name and address on the gun case, knew I was a guest there and returned it to me when we checked out."

Joe paused for a moment and then continued. "The gun had been wiped clean."

Voss didn't blink. "I always clean my gun thoroughly before I put it away. I didn't notice that it had been wiped clean because it always is after I use it. It certainly never occurred to me that it might have been used in a crime in the meantime. And indeed we don't know that it has, do we?"

"We won't know until after the ballistic reports come back."

Joe didn't mention that, to get a match for the gun, they would need to find the bullets in the woods or in the body first. And as far as I knew, they still hadn't found either bullets or their casings.

Without giving anything away, Joe changed the subject. "Can you tell me, Mr. Voss, what you were doing during the hours of the race on Saturday morning?"

"I went out to watch the first wave of skiers leave. That's always a thrilling sight. Then I went back to Lakewood and had breakfast with my wife. You can check the times with her."

"We were told by several people that you're a very good cross-country skier and that you'd signed up to ski in this year's Birkebeiner."

"I changed my mind. My wife isn't an outdoor person, and I decided to spend the day with her."

"Tell me about the rest of your day."

"I thought I had. After breakfast, we headed for her father's place for a little shooting."

"Your wife was with you?"

"Of course. Just ask her. We were never apart all day except for the short time I spent that morning watching the first waves of skiers start out."

"She went out in the woods shooting with you?"

Voss was now visibly upset. "Of course not. She hates guns. But I'm sure she could hear the sounds of shooting from the Walker's Lodge."

Joe took a moment to study his notes and I watched Hy. He was breathing harder and sweating a little bit. But he still had a cold impatient look on his face.

"We talked to several people who said it had been your intention to ski this year's race, that you had talked about it for months."

"Move on, Sheriff. I've already told you I changed my mind."

"Must have been last minute. One of the Birkebeiner officials at the start of the race states that he saw you there, wearing your skis, racing suit, and your numbered bib."

"Naturally I was wearing all of that. As a racer, I knew I would be allowed to get in close at the beginning of the race and see things first hand. Without gear and a bib, I wouldn't have a chance. When they took off, I turned around and left. The officials didn't have time to notice that, I suppose."

Joe ignored the sarcasm and said, "Let's talk about this morning. May I ask why you were late in getting to Telemark for our appointment?"

"My wife was a little tired. I let her sleep in. I was sure you'd still be here whenever we got here."

"People noticed that you were dressed for the city but wearing great big boots and that your jacket was covered in snow. Got a reason for that?"

"I don't need a reason. I assume this is still a somewhat free country, and I can wear anything I goddam please."

Joe smiled. "That's all the questions for now, Mr. Voss."

"When can I get back to town?"

"I hope you'll be able give us a little more of your time. We'll have your statement typed up. We'll want you to read it carefully and sign it."

"I hope I won't have to bother my lawyers with all this, Sheriff Bear."

Joe gave him one of those blank, cold looks that lawmen do so well and replied softly, "I hope so too, Mr. Voss, for your sake."

The questioning had turned up some surprises. Hy had a gun. The gun had gone missing at a convenient time. It could have been stolen and used for the murder on the ski hill at the Birkebeiner. Or Hy could have skied into the woods where he had left his rifle and used it himself and then thrown it out on the highway on the way back to Lakewood. Either way, it was going to be damn hard to prove. Voss was smarter than I'd known.

Of course, creative people in advertising have always liked to think that account executives, money men and media buyers are brain dead. Why would anyone go into the fun ad business just to count or make money? Looks like we were wrong about Hy.

The door opened and Mrs. Voss swept in, trailing her minks behind her. Seeing her close-up on the TV screen, I had to admit she was really beautiful in a good bones, good teeth, great hair, perfect skin kind of way. And her answers were really surprising.

Joe asked her, "I'd like to check some of the times Mr. Voss said he spent with you first. Saturday morning, early?"

"Waste of time. I never pay a lot of attention to Hy in the morning. He could have been there or not. I seem to remember the national news was on. Hy was probably swearing at the liberals. But that could have been any time, any day. He does it often to annoy me. My family has always been Democrat."

"Can you tell me what you were doing the morning of the Birkebeiner, Mrs. Voss?"

"Please, call me Katherine. I had breakfast in my room. I was reading a good book, *Walking the Rez Road* by Jim Northrup. Hy was getting ready to race. I assume he told you that."

"He said you had breakfast and spent the entire day together."

"That's typical of Hy. He talks and talks until he gets himself into a real jam. Then he threatens to go to the lawyers."

Joe continued with the questioning, and Katherine Voss answered readily and intelligently. She sounded truthful too, a rarity in the Pirelli group. It got a little personal when he asked about motives for harming Mary Dee.

Katherine paused a second and then said, "I have heard that Mary Dee is a truly awful human being. She has insulted, harmed, alienated or slept with almost everyone at Pirelli's Pasta and the agency. Probably even Hy, although he's usually too self-protective to let a tramp like that get anything on him. I've heard Mary Dee tries to get sexually involved with nearly everyone who can help her get ahead. I can't prove any of this, and I don't really care. I get my information from my husband's secretary. Talk to her when you get to Minneapolis."

When Joe dug all the answers and opinions he could, he asked her to wait for her testimony to be typed and to sign it. Then he thanked her and told her she'd be free to return to town if she wished.

"I don't wish to return right away," Katherine said. "I've been looking for a woman here, a member of the Coeur d'Alene tribe by marriage to a man named Bear. She's from the Mille Lac tribe and her tribal name is Doe Running."

I could see Joe was stunned, but he answered quickly. "Doe Running is my mother. I can help you get in touch with her if you tell me why you want to meet her."

"She's famous. Her knowledge of Native American herbs and healing is legendary. I'm very interested in that. Actually, I'm trying to write a book about it. And Doe Running and I are related. We had the same great-grandmother."

Joe laughed. "I'll give your name, address and number to my mother. I'm sure she'll call you if she's in town. And she usually is during Birkebeiner week."

"Megwetch, Sheriff Bear."

"*Megwetch*, cousin."

I put my head down and counted my sins. Prejudice was the big one. I had ignored Katherine Voss and just assumed she was a snob, a dummy and no one I'd be interested in. And she turned out to be terrific.

The next thing to come bubbling up from my sinful soul was, of course, jealousy. Joe thought she was wonderful. Any fool, meaning me, could see that. And they were related but not so close as to be a problem. And she'd be meeting his mother.

Coming in third, was pride, although mine had been deflated enormously. I thought Joe couldn't possibly solve these murders without my giving him background on the players. Turns out the secretarial pool at the agency had years more experience in the real scuttlebutt. Joe might not need me at all. I was going to change. Become a better person. Really, I meant it.

# CHAPTER NINETEEN

THE QUESTIONING WENT ON ALL DAY Monday and until noon Tuesday. When the last suspect left, I heard Joe's bossy voice on the monitor ordering me to come into the interrogation room so we could compare notes. I was too tired to start one of my Hear Me Roar I Am Woman rants so I just agreed.

As I came out of the room, a bony arm ending in prehensile red talons grabbed me. It was the unlovely Mary Dee, and she came slithering closer, breathing fire. "We've been talking about you. Everyone knows you were listening in on our interviews. And everyone's boiling mad. If I were you, Dwarf, I'd be careful going out at night. Hell, anytime you're alone, better keep looking over your shoulder." And with a wild cackle she was gone. It shook me up enough to tell Joe about it.

All he said was, "Nonsense. If there's one thing in place, it's security for all of you. There'll be no more murders. Your being in on the testimony would upset only the guilty one. To do anything to you would point the finger at him or her."

It seemed like a pretty flimsy plan for keeping me safe. Obviously, Joe was anxious to get on with our conclusions. "You know these people, Amy. You have a better chance of deciding if their testimony is within character or not. And I'm hoping you've got a pretty good idea of which ones could possibly be guilty. Did I ask the questions you wanted answered?"

"For the most part," I said icily, "but I thought you were pretty easy on Mrs. Voss."

Joe was puzzled. "You think she could be guilty? What's her motivation?"

I sorted through all the teeming, jealous thoughts in my brain and came up with such a loser. "She could have been having an affair with someone. And Mary Dee found out about it."

"Who could it be? You told me Katherine Voss hardly ever comes near your agency."

"It might have been a sudden passion."

"Who did you have in mind?"

"Anyone. She's obviously not getting it on with her husband. She's desperate. Maybe it was Geno or Mac. Maybe it was even Stephano."

Joe laughed so hard at this he almost fell out of his chair. "I'll be damned. You're jealous of the beautiful Mrs. Voss. I consider this a very good sign of your growing passion for me."

"As usual," I said, "your enormous conceit has caused you to make another horrendous mistake. You also let your lust for some suspects blind your judgment."

Joe kept laughing as he asked me what it would take to make us friends again. I naturally chose food. He picked up the phone and ordered two giant burgers with everything, an order of fries and a hot fudge malt, all for me. He asked a deputy to go and pick it up.

Leering, Joe said, "The best combination. A hot-blooded, jealous woman with a hearty appetite. A big appetite in one area usually promises a big appetite in other physical areas too."

I gave Joe my superbly chilling frozen face look and began going though my list. I started with my notes on Peter's testimony. "I thought you might suspect Peter. I heard some little rat told you about Peter's angry rant about Mary Dee after the Birke."

"He was a long shot possibility. I was also told that rant included his loudly spoken and heartfelt desire to see Mary Dee dead."

"But remember, it turned out his partner, Mark Rollings, was with Peter the whole day of the race and also during the entire evening party. So he had no chance to shoot the skier or harm poor Angela."

"Unless," Joe said, "they're both lying."

"You don't know Peter. He couldn't hurt anyone. He was just blowing off steam. He wouldn't even do that with anyone but me or Mark."

"Okay. Scratch Peter for now. Who else do you think could have done it?"

"I'd rather start with the ones I don't think could be guilty. I was really disappointed to have to drop some of the people on this list. No new clues, no surprises. I never considered Mrs. Smythe-Larson in spite the nausea I feel whenever I think of her."

"How very fair-minded of you," Joe said dryly.

"Nor do I really think Mama Pirelli could have committed any of the crimes personally. However, if she hired help, I'd be willing to bet we'll never find out. Next, Chuck and Virginia Pylon are my good friends and, therefore, innocent. Quit shaking your head. It isn't just my prejudice. Actually they wouldn't have had a chance unless they were both lying as they swore they'd been together during the entire pertinent times."

"Again, this is true unless they're both lying," Joe said. "And remember, Virginia Pylon was good and drunk Sunday night. She fell asleep, my deputy told me. Maybe she was drinking hard all weekend. She might have slept through Chuck's absence."

"Granted, they might be in it together," I agreed. "But Virginia would have had to be drunk for forty-eight hours in a row for Chuck to have gotten away with murder. Couldn't have happened. She'd have died herself."

I took a breath, and Joe didn't interrupt me, so I went on. "Let's continue with my real outsiders. Angela Krajak was one of the victims and Lucia Pirelli would never have been involved in her father's murder. Therefore, each of those two is innocent of at least one of the crimes. I'm firmly convinced that the same person is guilty of both murders plus the attempted murder of Angela. So I consider all the people I've mentioned to be non-starters."

"I'll probably look at your friends a little harder than you did, Amy, but for now, let's get on to the starters."

"My biggest possibility was Mac Larson. My biggest regret is that I can't see a reason to jail him today. He's such a natural. I think a killer has to be totally self-absorbed, and I've never met anyone more so than Mac. But he's cunning. I don't remember that he said anything today that you could pin the murders on him for."

Joe nodded his head in agreement. "He said he'd gotten drunk Friday night, and that's why he had such a bad race time in the Birkebeiner in spite of his amazing skiing ability."

"He claims to have been so upset at finding poor Angela that he got drunk again Saturday night, which led to a long sleep on Sunday with his cell phone turned off."

Joe said, "No one saw him, and he claims he didn't hear the hotel phone ring at all. We can check with the Telemark staff, but it's the kind of alibi that's really hard to prove or disprove."

"Let me do the rest of my list," I said. "Although I don't see a for-sure murderer at this point, there are some possibilities. Geno Pirelli finished the race with a great time. He was one of the top hundred racers. He wouldn't have had time to shoot the skier. This is too bad because I think he's been involved with

Mary Dee. Actually, I'm pretty sure he's been involved with every woman he can con in our five-state area. And Mary Dee is an always-available and easy playmate. When the fun was over, she'd know how vulnerable Geno would be with both his jealous wife and controlling mother. Mary Dee could make all sorts of demands if she had the goods on him. So Geno might have had a strong motive. But, unfortunately, he couldn't have done it."

"But couldn't he be a possible suspect for Stephano and Angela?"

"I doubt it. Geno is charming but bone-lazy. I can't see him going to the trouble of killing people off. He'd just pay them off. But he doesn't have an alibi for Angela or for Stephano. He could have done either one. I can't imagine his motive for Angela. She isn't the kind of woman who would interest him. He probably disliked Stephano on general principles but not enough to kill him. Everyone knows Stephano just follows Mama's orders."

"I get it," Joe agreed. "Geno might dislike Stephano for being a snitch but that's not personal. Nor did Stephano appear dangerous enough for Geno to warrant murdering him. We'll leave him on the list but personally, I think our best suspect right now, based solely on the interviews, is Mary Dee."

I was thrilled to hear Joe say what I wanted to be true. "I'd love for it to be Mary Dee because she is the most loathsome creature I know."

Joe nodded. "I try hard not to let personal feelings enter into my professional decisions, but I must say, she is a bad piece of work. She wandered off during the race and lied about finishing it. I don't believe she was out there and not one video camera spotted her at the finish. We have several, from every angle, in the finish area, and she's not in a single one. Nor was she spotted at Seeley, the halfway point, and they had a raft of cameras on the skiers there. I also think she lied about the bib and what she told you as she skied off. Am I right?"

How could I have doubted that Joe would believe me? Besides the fact that he was trying now and then to enjoy carnal knowledge of my person, he was also bright enough to see Mary Dee for the maggot liar she was. There was still a scintilla of doubt, of course. While I considered Mary Dee to have the right personality for a murderess and the right opportunity to kill the skier, what about the other crimes?

I said, "I don't think we can put the cuffs on her yet, Sheriff Bear. There are some minor points you have to explore first. I don't really think Mary Dee, big horse that she is, could lift Angela into the chair on the ski lift or put a very dead Stephano into the trunk of a car."

"You're right, Amy. I'm glad you didn't let dislike color your judgment."

"Not entirely. I still hope she's guilty. All we have to do is find out how Mary Dee could have moved two bodies around before you shoot her into the slammer. She could have had help. I still consider her suspect number one. Granted she could have gotten help from her current lover, whomever that might be, with little things. But help with two murders? That's a long prison sentence. She's hardly worth a traffic ticket."

"Got that right." Joe smiled. "So let's go on. We haven't talked about Mr. Voss, the man with the gun and no alibi for the first shooting."

I nodded and thought for a moment. "Hy looks good for the murder of the skier, and he might have tried to murder Angela, but I don't think he would have recognized her on the trail. They never cross paths at the agency. Also, he didn't stay at Telemark. He and his wife were at Lakewoods, and she was probably with him all Saturday night. The next day, he wouldn't have had much time for killing Stephano and putting his body in the trunk. He was with his wife and her family all day, shooting on his father-in-law's estate. He's out of the running for Stephano."

"Maybe. Maybe we just haven't come up with a way he might have done it. Put your mind on that, Amy. Now let's take a break and think about pleasanter things for a few moments."

I smiled my dead fox smile and said, "Aren't you forgetting someone? Mrs. Voss could have done all three just as easily as her husband. Her sole alibi for the time of the skier's death was that she was reading a good book. Now I'm a fan of literature, but that's pretty slim."

Joe looked amused but told me to go on and build my case if I could.

I didn't really want to but I had to show him it wasn't just jealousy but keen-eyed, impartial, reasoning. "Well, she certainly didn't sound like she loved Mary Dee. So that could have been the motivation for the first crime. The other two were to cover up the first murder. She probably got Hy to help her move the bodies around. After all, if he had been having at it with Mary Dee, he owed his wife some help with the cover-ups."

"You could be right. And that takes us to the end of your list, right?"

"It does. I believe we have four viable suspects counting Hy Voss. The Big Four are Geno Pirelli, Mac Larson, Hy Voss, and Mary Dee Frank."

"We'll concentrate on all four. This pretty much wraps up what we can do here. If you can wait around a few hours while I set things up, I can drive you down to the Twin Cities, you lucky girl. We're taking the case down there, and we'll be guests of the Hennepin County Sheriff's Office. They're providing us with space and office equipment."

157

Tempting. Very tempting. I wanted to go with Joe, but I really needed a faster ride back to Minneapolis before I burned my last bridge. I hadn't heard from Ryan, and that was worrying me plenty. I might have strained our romance to the breaking point this time. Nor had I returned any of my mother's or brothers' phone calls. It was time to face some extremely discordant music.

# CHAPTER TWENTY

I TOLD JOE I'D GET BACK TO HIM and went upstairs to call Ryan. No answer. I called my folks. When my mother answered, she sounded pretty cool. She reminded me that I was due home for my brother Mike's birthday at seven, that the whole family was coming, and she had also invited Ryan.

"You'd better get down here, Amy. I know Ryan has something important to talk to you about, and it seems you've been too busy with your sleuthing to listen. He's leaving to-morrow on a trip, so you'll have a chance to see him before he goes."

My stomach hurt after we hung up. I was damn happy to hear that Ryan had said I was detecting and nothing else. He didn't rat me out even when I was behaving badly. But Ryan's not telling me about a big trip was awful. I suppose he'd tried. That was the big news I hadn't had time to listen to. Tonight he probably just wanted to say goodbye forever. I couldn't let that happen. I loved Ryan. I needed to find a ride home and fast.

As I packed, I tried to figure what person would be the safest to ask for a ride home. I wasn't any too anxious to drive home alone with a possible murderer. And they were the only ones I knew that were still in Hayward.

If I wanted to get home by seven, I'd better call one of them. I decided to call Hy Voss and his wife. I figured there might be safety in the number two. Unfortunately, when their car arrived, just Hy was in it. Katherine had decided to stay in

Hayward to meet Joe's mother. I was alone with Hy, and he didn't look happy see me.

"Been busy snitching I hear, Amy, helping that sheriff put one of your co-workers in jail. Someone saw you coming out of a room at Telemark where you had been listening to our testimony and telling him about all of us. I just hope you didn't get too creative. Could be dangerous."

And that was the last bit of happy talk all the way home. It wasn't any jollier at my folks' either. Ryan hadn't arrived, but the Irish Mafia were lined up like avenging angels. My brothers have always thought they had the right to boss me around in the mistaken idea that I was hopelessly stupid and fatally careless.

Mike, the oldest, was a St. Paul cop, and Kevin, the middle one, a priest. Fitzgerald, the youngest, not counting me, was a lawyer, just like my dad, who was now a judge. They were all big, stubborn and totally convinced I'd be lost without their constant advice. And tonight they were not happy with me. Getting shot at, they told me, turned out to be my fault some-how, and staying to help with the questioning, dumber than dumb. Worst of all, I hadn't come home with Ryan when he came up to get me. They all liked Ryan, probably more than they did me, if truth be told.

Ryan didn't arrive until right before dinner, so we had no time to talk. He was smiling and happy, so he wasn't as upset with me as the brothers. He slid into to his chair, leaned over and gave me a sweet little kiss, the kind brothers approve of.

After dinner, during which I suffered agonies of curiosity, Ryan said he had to leave as he had an early plane to catch. "If you want to leave now, Amy, I can give you a ride to your place and we can catch up on the way."

We loaded my skis and gear into his car and took off, but Ryan wouldn't discuss his trip until we got to my place, telling me it was a bit complicated. We settled in, and I got us each a drink and then Ryan unloaded.

"Actually, Amy, this isn't just a trip. My law firm is sending me to London to work on the Big Ben Insurance account, one of our biggest clients. I'll be living in London. They've found me a flat there, and I've sublet my apartment here."

My blood turned cold. "This is quite sudden. Why didn't you tell me?"

"I did, Amy. I told you about the possibility six months ago. When I asked you to marry me this month, I told you they'd offered me the position. You assumed I'd turn it down. I didn't want to. I really wanted this assignment. It's a big promotion and they're going to make me a partner if I perform well over there."

"You could have talked to me. Really talked. I'd have listened."

"I've been trying to talk to you about our future all year. I want you to come with me. I can't think of anything more fun than the two of us let loose in England together. But I couldn't get you to really take it seriously or to convince you to pack in the agency job and fly away with me. My other plan involved my going over until Christmas and then coming back for our wedding."

"What wedding? I thought we'd agreed to wait a couple more years. We're so young. We're not ready."

"I think I'm ready. But you've said you're not. This week you finally convinced me that we are too young. Right now I don't think marriage is a good idea. This week I also thought it might be a good time for me to get on with my life."

I felt that remark hit me like a knife in my stomach. "I don't want you to go on without me. Why didn't you tell me, when you came up to Hayward, that you were leaving this quickly?"

"I didn't get the word until I got home. The rush is because Parliament has just passed some new laws about insurance that affect our client. They need counsel on site right away. I either had to go immediately or turn the job down. I've been busy ever since, packing and finding a tenant for my condo. And you've been a little busy yourself, Amy."

I felt a wave of shame and sorrow. This was as close as Ryan had ever come to really criticizing my behavior or me. He knew I got enough of that from the brothers. I swallowed hard and said, "I know. That's true. And I'm very, very sorry. But I never thought you'd go off forever without me."

"I'm not going off forever without you. I'll probably be back home during the holidays. I just think you need more time. I'm willing to try some other things and wait until you're ready."

The next morning, I took Ryan to the airport. Before he boarded, he turned and said, "I love you, Amy. I always will. And when you feel ready, come to me. I'll be waiting."

I drove home, crying all the way. I hadn't been without Ryan since I was seven and he was eleven. Life without him seemed impossible. He said he'd wait for me. But what or who were the other things he would be trying in London while he waited? A parade of beautiful Brits? Long, naughty weekends at stately homes? Weekends in Paris with gorgeously tall and very smart women barristers?

I knew I had better think up a great campaign to keep Ryan away from all of them. Naturally they'd all want him. Ryan was great looking, smart, rich and nice. But they'd have to look elsewhere. Ryan was mine.

# CHAPTER TWENTY-ONE

W HAT A DOG DAY WEDNESDAY IS means it's right in the stinking middle of the week with two whole days left to the weekend. It was always bad but this one promised to be the worst Wednesday on record for me. I hadn't slept. I was hung over from the emotion of the night before with Ryan. Well, I wasn't going to think about that.

I was going to pretend it hadn't happened for now. A deep pretense like my pal Gerald who hated flying and just pretended he was on a very long bridge when the plane was over an ocean. Worked for him.

Coffee always helped. Starting to feel a little less like a birdcage bottom, I turned on the radio while I got dressed for work. The sadistic voice of the happy weatherman sang out ten degrees below zero weather with a minus-forty-degree wind chill. Minnesota weather featured lots of wind chill information as a way to punish us for living here and provide amusement for the rest of the country. Someday I would meet that happy weatherman at a party or a poetry reading and then there would be trouble.

Actually the leaden skies and dirty snow weren't the main reason I was anxious about going to work. Mary Dee and Hy Voss had both warned me that I was no longer a very popular co-worker after the group caught me listening in on their testimonies. My two BFFs weren't going to be any help. Peter might be angry, thinking that I had told Joe about his Mary Dee rant the afternoon of the Birkebeiner. And Angela wasn't back at work yet. I would be friendless, and I hated that. Still, I had go in to the agency as Miss Uncongeniality, and take the heat.

I really wanted to see if I could solve these murders. I thought I had a good chance because I'd read almost every good mystery there was. Plus I really knew this cast of suspect characters. So I gritted my teeth, grabbed my huge down coat and went bravely to work.

I got to the agency almost on time. My boss, Chuck Pylon smiled and seemed glad to see me but that was probably because there were lots of Pirelli Pasta jobs due by Friday and he needed a writer.

I said carefully, "Chuck, you know, I hope, that anything you've ever told me will never be shared with anyone. It's in the vault forever."

"I appreciate that, Amy, but I wouldn't be worried if you had told Sheriff Bear about what I told you. I don't think he'd think that was a big enough reason to snuff two people and try for a third. I know I'm not guilty and neither is Virginia. All I'm worried about is that she'll find out about my high school stupidity."

"Never from me, Chuck. But I still think you should tell her. Secrets are hell on a relationship. When you're as close as the two of you are, the other person can smell a lie. And her imagination is going to come up with something lots worse than the truth."

"You're right. I know you're right. But I just don't know what to say. I worry she might not have married me if she'd known."

"You were young and she's smart and fair. She may be hurt but she isn't going to leave you or even punish you. Take my word, I know women."

Chuck laughed, "That's right, you've had all these years of experience with marriage, haven't you? Oh, no, that's right, not yet. But you do have almost twenty-three years of living experience."

"Make that almost twenty-four years and sensitive people don't need a million years before they understand the human heart."

"I give. Anyway, better get with Peter on those newspaper coupon ads for Pirelli Pasta. They're due the end of the week."

Ugh. Was there a worse assignment than those little twenty-five-cent-off-coupon ads? I don't want to know about it if there is. They are creativity killing, boring, and crammed with disclaimers in tiny type. Clients loved them. Unfortunately they worked. It was time to get them done. I went to find Peter and to face the music about my listening in. I just hoped he wasn't too upset with me.

Peter and I always worked together, and it was a ball to work with someone as creative as he was, and one with no puffball ego. We sat around and traded ideas and sometimes I came up with the visual idea, his job, or he got the clever headline, my job. Mary Dee had been to Chuck a hundred times claiming we were laughing and hooting and just wasting time. We weren't. That was just our way of working and it had paid off. Last May, we had a Best of Show from the Minneapolis-St. Paul Ad Club and a runner-up Cleo from *The Show* in New York.

When I came into his office, Peter was working on a gorgeous brochure for a local decorator. I waited for him to save his work. When he was finished, he turned to me and said, "I know you didn't rat on me, Amy, so quit squirming. I think that little waste of space, Mac Larson, did. He was hanging around you all night like you had some secret he wanted to know, with his face all scrunched up."

"No, I think that's just how he looks when he's horny. Don't gag. I don't actually know this for a fact and never, never will try to find out if it's true."

"Maybe so but I think he really needed to hear what we were saying."

"That's just Mac. Always snuffling around trying to get anything on anybody he can use to his advantage. Don't worry about your threat to Mary Dee. I'd be willing to bet that almost all Voss and Pylon people, who aren't managerial level, have wished her permanently erased more than once and have all said so out loud and in front of witnesses."

Peter didn't look convinced. "But I was the only one heard saying it during the party. The same day someone took a shot at her."

"Took a shot at *me*, actually, Peter dear. But again, don't worry. I've explained all to the law, and they're quite, quite convinced that you're not guilty of anything but a temper tantrum. And after meeting Mary Dee for themselves, they think you're a saint not to have had lots more and lots worse tantrums."

"Who do you think did it, Amy?"

"I don't know yet, but I will. I've come up with a swell idea. It carries the tiniest soupçon of risk, but if I tell you about it, any risk disappears. Once a second person knows, the killer wouldn't dare harm me. My plan for cornering a killer is, therefore, safe, quite easy, yet brilliant and hopefully foolproof."

"Amy, you're not going to try and deal with a real cold-blooded killer. Leave it to the police. Or at least get them involved."

"If I thought the police could do it, I'd let them. But I don't think they can. I know these people, and I think I can find the murderer."

"Without getting murdered yourself? Well, what's your big idea?"

"Promise not to tell anyone? Put your hand on you heart and swear. Good. The plan is very simple. I'm just going to poke a few sticks into a few hornet's nests and see what comes out."

"You're going to lay traps for a killer? Don't do this, Amy. I won't help you. You'll be killed. And you'll take me with you. Where do you think you're getting these sticks anyway? You don't really know who's guilty, do you?"

"Of course not. But when the maddened hornet comes out to play, I'll know."

Peter groaned and sat with his head in his hands as I laid out my plot. I wanted to see the Big Four who were on Joe's and my possible suspects list. I would approach each one with a clever lie, one that fit them perfectly. The lie would be about something I might have discovered or overheard. After all, they knew that I had been the ears and eyes for the law and knew lots of things they didn't. That's why they were so mad at me. My clever lie had to be believable but not gospel yet. By the end of the day, I wanted to get four people worried and one of them really worried. I'd be careful not to be alone with any one of them. I could keep myself safe. And Peter, in spite of his moaning, would probably help me.

I had thought about working with Joe but I knew he'd be too cautious to let me try. And I certainly was not going to let fear stop me. I was hunting a murderer.

I decided to start with Mac mainly because it was so much fun to get him steamed. That would mean going up two floors. Pylon & Voss Advertising was laid out with three full floors in the IDS tower on Nicollet Mall in downtown Minneapolis, the tallest building in town and still the most prestigious.

The people who actually did most of the work for the agency were on the forty-seventh floor. There we created the only thing an agency really had to sell—ideas. The staff included writers, artists, designers, production staff, and traffic. The newest department had an ever-growing number of Internet experts. Our floor also had the library and a small kitchen for testing product.

The forty-eighth floor had the support staff — media buyers and planners, television and radio production, research, public and media relations, and marketing.

This floor also had my favorite spot, the Media Library. It contains several copies of every TV and radio show that contains an ad of one or more of our clients. I loved some of the old sit-coms, and if I kept the volume down, I could spend many happy hours in there. It also had copies of what seemed to be every magazine that was published.

Forty-nine, the top floor, had all the suits. Those were the people who called on the clients, most of whom were account or client managers. Account execs spent their days in a constant panic about what date they had promised finished ads to the client, and what date they had told creative to have them ready. The two dates had never matched in the history of advertising.

This floor also included the brass except for V.P. Chuck Pylon who stayed down with his creative teams. Human Resources, The Money Men, and Legal all had large plush offices up there.

It was time to get on to the first suspect. I thought of a dandy lie for Mac and went to poke a stick at him. Luckily, he seemed fairly pleased to see me.

"Get out," he said.

"Mac, don't be rude to an old friend."

"You're a slimy, tattle-telling little spy, Amy. My interest in you as a possible life partner is gone. Which I wish you were."

"I'll try to bear up being crossed off your mate list, Mac, but do you really want to break your mother's heart? She seemed to really like and approve of me."

Mac came zinging out of his chair. "Mother always thought of you as a Bingo playing, mackerel-snapper and a snotty nobody with middle-class manners. I let your somewhat obvious charms blind me. Well, not any more. Get out."

"My obvious charms being my father, the judge, my brother the number one criminal lawyer in town, my brother the cop who knows everyone, and my brother the priest from a large parish which might get you votes if you married a Catholic?"

"Get out," he snarled, "or I'll call security."

"Mac, I came to do you a favor, to warn you."

"Now why would you want to do me a favor?"

"We've been friends." I cooed, batting my eyelashes. "I still consider you a friend in spite of your atrocious manners this morning."

"Your warning better be damn good. Spill."

"You were seen skiing off the trail, right before the Grandma Hill where that girl was shot. The person who noticed you says you skied way into the woods, and he remembered because it was such a strange thing to do."

"I had to go to the bathroom if it's any of your business. That's why I had such a lousy time in the race this year."

"Jeez, for a guy peeing takes about ten seconds. How could that ruin your time?"

"No, no it wasn't that quick. It was the other."

"The other what?"

"Oh, for God's sake, it was—ah—diarrhea. I was nervous."

I couldn't help it. I roared with laughter. The idea of Mac bare-assed, on skis, in three feet of snow was a mental image meant for a frat house comedy. "Well," I said finally, wiping my eyes, "that doesn't really provide you with an alibi you know."

"There is evidence out there in the snow. Proof I'm not lying."

"It was snowing all weekend Mac. Do you really think you could dig around and find your little pile of proof?"

"I don't know. I won't have to. I don't believe you anyway. You're just trying to rattle me. Who saw me?"

"I can't give you the name. I would, of course, but I promised not to."

"That's because there is no person who saw me. You made it up. You should be a little more careful, Amy. People hate snitches. I could sue you."

"Big threat, Mac. Do that and I'll have to play this conversation at the next office party," I said, pulling a little tape recorder out of my pocket. I was immediately sorry, I had done that. The look on Mac's face was enough to frighten the Red Army. His face went beet red, his eyes blazed, and his lips were stretched back so all his teeth were bared. He looked like a cornered rat.

I got up quickly and made for the door. As I left, I squeaked out, "You really can't take a joke, Mac. I wouldn't play the tape for anyone. But I will hang on to it. I'll just run along now. Remember, I tried to do you a favor. Bye now."

A little chastened, I slipped down to the Media Library to get my breath back and wait until my heart stopped trying to get out of my body. I knew Mac was the most selfish human alive, so into himself that he considered others only as small orbits floating around him in order to serve him somehow. But I hadn't really gotten used to the idea that he had the chutzpah to be a murderer. I saw the different Mac again just now. He looked like he would have killed me with pleasure, if we'd been alone.

When I had calmed down, I knew I couldn't hang out here reading magazines all day no matter how closely that matched my work style. I had three other murder prospects to scare with my clever lies. I could go back down to the creative department and find Mary Dee, but if I did that, Peggy, the traffic person, would see me and make me go to work. She was like a ferret. She could slip around the agency noiselessly, and she always found the slackers like me.

I had a better chance to avoid work if I stayed up here. I could try seeing Hy Voss. I would poke him with a couple sticks and try to get him stirred up enough to crack if he was guilty. I went up a flight, walked down the hall to the executive wing and stopped by the desk of Hy's secretary. I called her the Frozen Meringue.

"Marilyn, if he's not too busy right now I'd like a word with Mr. Voss."

"He's very busy," she said without looking away from her computer. "What do you want to see him about this morning?"

"It's a personal matter I want to share just with him."

"I doubt, Amy, that it's important enough to disturb him. I'll tell him you were here, if you'd like."

"I'd like it a lot more if you'd tell him I *am* here now. Let him make up his own mind whether or not I'm important enough to spend five minutes with."

With a pursing of her already razor-thin lips, Frozen Meringue picked up the phone and buzzed the inner office. She told Voss that I wished to see him with icy disapproval in every word. When he answered, she looked amazed. "He'll see you. Go right in."

Hy looked a lot more imposing behind his big desk than he had during the Birkebeiner. His face didn't register joy at my visit but neither did it have a murderous look. "Well, busy little Amy," he said. "What can I tell you today that you don't think you already know?"

"Oh, you're teasing me, Mr. Voss. I'm not here to get you to tell me anything. I'm here to tell you something I've overheard about the case."

"And you think I'd be interested because . . ."

"Because it's about your gun. I forgot to tell you what I overheard yesterday when you were kind enough to give me a ride home. Something I truly appreciated, by the way."

If I simpered any more I thought I'd have sugar dripping from my mouth. Hy wasn't buying it either but he was curious. He shifted in his chair and his eyes had gotten sharper. "So tell me," he ordered.

I stumbled ahead with my clever lies. "They've found a definite marking in the gun but the bullet was too smashed."

I could see and feel Hy relax. "However," I added, "they've sent it to an FBI lab in Washington that does remarkable work in ballistics, and they feel sure they'll be able to get a match. Also, there was a smudge on the trigger that they're hoping is a partial fingerprint. That should clear you of any suspicion."

"I wasn't aware I was under any suspicion. Are you saying that I am?"

"No, no of course not. But finding a witness who saw you on the sidelines during the race didn't help of course. He said you were all the way down the trail by Seeley, the halfway mark."

"I suppose a busy little person like you can tell me just who that person was who said they saw me?"

"I do remember the name, but I'm absolutely sworn to secrecy."

Hy leaned forward and fixed me with a very cold eye. "Do you want to know what I think Amy? I think you know zero, nada, zip, nothing. I think you've persuaded yourself that you're quite the little detective. You aren't. You have no training and little aptitude for that job. You think you know something but I'd bet you're wrong. Dead wrong. And here's fair warning for you. Don't mess in this. Stop these silly games with a killer. You're certain to be murdered if you don't. Now, get out."

Hy had never raised his voice but his look and tone were so lethal I felt icy sweat running down my back. And to add insult to fear, he picked up the phone, buzzed his secretary and said, "Marilyn, make a note. Tell payroll to deduct two days pay from Ms. Connolly's next check for the work she missed Monday and Tuesday. There was no good reason why she couldn't have been here both those days."

I had found out something that day about Hy Voss. He was a really mean man.

# CHAPTER TWENTY-TWO

T HINGS WERE GETTING A LOT MORE dramatic a lot faster than I had counted on, but I was not going to slink off scared. And it was only fair that I should give all four of my top prospects a chance to give themselves away. I certainly had managed to get a hornet's nest buzzing with both Mac and Hy Voss. Now it was time to poke at the other two, Geno and Mary Dee.

Geno was often at the agency but he wasn't today, so I went down to the creative floor to torment Mary Dee. Her door was closed. She didn't want company and particularly not me. I rapped just once and then quickly opened the door and went straight in before she could stop me. She had already pushed away from her desk, ready to leave. She looked terrible and mean and, when she saw me, even worse.

"Did you hear me say come in? I didn't and you're not welcome here. So get out, Dwarf, before I throw you out."

"Well, I am shocked, Mary Dee. I didn't expect thanks for bringing you news you should have but I did think you'd treat me with common courtesy. Oh, that's right. Courtesy is the only thing that isn't common about you."

"Look, you dumb pygmy, there isn't anything you could say that I want to hear. So I repeat, get out while you're still not bleeding."

"You need to hear this. I heard, well overheard, that you're a suspect and that you've moved way up on the list."

"You're bluffing. You don't know anything about a suspect list or where I am on it. Why would anyone in authority share info with a little nothing like you?"

"They didn't know they were sharing. I just overheard it. They thought the monitor in my room was turned off but it wasn't."

"So are you really going to tell me what you know? I don't believe it. Why would you do me a favor?"

It took me a while to come up with an answer to that, given the pure poison of our relationship since the day we'd first met. I finally said, "Co-workers should stick together in times of trouble. And while we are ah—not close friends—we do work together."

Mary Dee laughed and made a crude gesture with her middle finger, aimed at me.

"Actually," I said, "that wasn't a reason I thought you'd swallow. I just said it to be polite. Here's the truth. I want to trade with you. I'll give you my news. You lay off Peter and Angela. No more threatening to fire them, no more calling them Queer Boy and Scarface. Do this and I'll tell you why you've moved up the suspect list."

"Okay, I agree. Get on with it."

"Swear to it."

"I swear. This had better be good."

"They've found traces of makeup on Angela's jacket. And Angela doesn't wear makeup because it just makes her scars look worse. They also found a small lipstick stain. It isn't a color or brand of lipstick that Angela ever wears, but they seem to think it matches one of the colors you often wear."

"Big hairy deal. It isn't mine, and if it were, all I'd have to do is throw away all my makeup and get new. I take back my swear."

"That's so typical of you, Mary Dee," I said hotly. "You're such a cheat. I haven't even gotten to the part where they think they might have gotten some DNA. Enough to put you in the slammer, I hope."

I'd been watching her face change from pink to red to purple. I was so fascinated by the color changes, I failed seeing her pick up and throw her cup full of coffee. I did see it in time to duck to one side and watch it go by and smash to the floor. The heavy cup didn't hurt me but it could have. It was aimed at my head. Her reckless behavior scared me. Most people lived by unspoken, societal rules. Mary Dee didn't. She did what she wanted, had no boundaries. I got out before she could regroup and have another go at me.

As long as I was in the art department, I stopped by Angela's office. It was empty and forlorn looking, with everything tidied up or put away. It looked like she wouldn't ever come back. My conscience came to life with a bang and gave me a good kick for selfishness. I hadn't called or seen Angela once since I heard she'd left the hospital. I kept checking up on her with Joe, but I failed to do the things a real friend did — phone calls, flowers, visits, and, best of all, food.

I sat right down, whipped out my cell and studied the agency personnel list. I found Angela's entry of who to call in case of an emergency. It was a number in New Prague, a Czech town about thirty miles from Minneapolis where Angela had lived all her life with her grandparents. Poor Angela started life unwanted.

Her mother had left her at the hospital when she was born, leaving the old couple to care for her. I called, hoping that Angela would be there and answer the phone. Neither of her grandparents spoke enough English for us to have a conversation, and my Czech lacked, well, everything.

I soon heard an old voice saying, "Who is please?"

"Hello, Mrs. Krajak, it's Amy Connolly. May I speak to Angela please?"

"Angela? Is Angela?"

"No, no, Mrs. Krajak . . . it's Amy."

"Wait."

I heard the phone drop to the floor with a clang and then lots of loud talk in Czech. That was followed by a very long wait. Finally, the phone was picked up again, and I heard the voice of their next-door neighbor, a very nice lady I'd met last time I came home with Angela. She often was called over to translate for the Krajaks.

"Hello, Angela. Why in heaven's name didn't you call? Your grandparents have been worried sick about you."

"It isn't Angela, Mrs. Havel. It's her friend Amy Connolly. Where is Angela?"

"Why, she's back at work already. She recovered fast and got a clean bill of health from her doctor yesterday afternoon. One of her friends or co-workers came to pick her up this morning. You can look for her at the advertising agency where she works. I can't recall the name offhand. Anyway, she's in Minneapolis."

I begged her to tell me what the co-worker looked like. She hadn't seen him. She asked the Krajaks but they hadn't seen the driver either. I tried to keep my voice calm as I thanked Mrs. Havel and hung up the phone.

I looked around Angela's empty office and felt a wave of fear so strong that I shook all over. Where was she? Who had come to pick her up? I needed Joe. I had to get through to him right away and get the police to start looking for her. I punched in the number at the Hennepin County Sheriff's Office that Joe had given me before I left Hayward. A voice introduced himself as Sergeant Olsen and promised to get Joe on the line right away. It seemed like an hour before I heard his voice.

I told him about Angela's disappearance with the mysterious co-worker. I started to cry and said, "She's in trouble. I feel it. If she's not okay it's my fault. Why didn't I check up on her? Why didn't I find out what she was going to do? It's your fault too. I trusted you to look out for her and what did you do? You let her disappear."

"You don't know she's disappeared. Maybe she went off to be with a friend. At first, we had someone with her round the clock. After that we did keep tabs on her, but she's an adult, free to go where she wishes. We tried very hard to get some or any information about the accident from her but failed. That bump on her head must have been just in the right place. She doesn't remember a thing."

"So you just pushed her out all alone?"

"Of course not." Joe let out an exasperated sigh. He spoke calmly as if to an over-excited child. "We took her to her grandparents in New Prague. We assumed she'd be well cared for there. We alerted the New Prague police, and they did regular drive-bys and also checked up by phone several times a day. We've let everyone of the suspects know that she doesn't remember anything. All of this should keep her safe from any more assaults. She's okay, Amy. We'll find her."

"She isn't okay. I just know she isn't. I want you to drop what you're doing and go out and find her."

"Calm down, Amy. I can't leave. I have a big crew of Wisconsin and Minnesota cops here. We're checking up on the Pirelli family, their business and your agency business and people. We've mountains of information to go through—business deals, banking records for possible embezzlements, investments, wills, and inheritances. Plus we've had almost a thousand calls from people who say they know something about one or another of the murders. Most of them are thrill seekers or nut cases, but every one has to be checked. Someone's going to have some real information for us sooner or later."

"What can you do right now? There must be something," I demanded.

"I'll alert the Minneapolis and New Prague police departments now. And I'll keep a constant check on the search, I promise."

"Okay. I have to trust you. But please put in motion all you can to find Angela. You just have to find her. My ESP tells me that she's in big, big trouble."

"I promise. I'd like to see you later to give you a report on the search and to find out if you've heard or suspected anything new with the people in your office. In the meantime," Joe added. "Do not discuss this with anyone at all, even someone you think you'd trust with your life. Because if it is the wrong person, it will be your life."

"I can take care of myself. I'm not a child or an idiot," I said witheringly.

"On the contrary, you are a child and you've been acting like an idiot about safety. Please, stay out of it. Things are getting more dangerous by the minute. I'll be at your place as soon as possible, but it will be late, nine-thirty or ten. Is that okay?"

"Yes, please come," I said. I gave him the address and hung up. Then I stayed in Angela's dark office and worried and prayed. After that I had a spell of good old guilt.

I hadn't exactly lied to Joe, but I'd avoided telling him about the hornets I had attempted to annoy to the point of doing something wrong and getting caught.

I went down to my floor, and Peggy caught me. She said she had looked everywhere for me and was quite cross. I promised her the copy in plenty of time to get a layout done. Luckily, it was a job that required no creative thought but it had to be done carefully and there were always tons of small print rules to include. I took the copy in to traffic when I finished, and then wandered around the creative department making small talk with anyone still talking to me.

When I got back to my own office, there was a pleasant surprise waiting for me.

Some pal had brought me a large Caribou's take-away container that just had to be either a crisp biscotti or a meltingly delicious big muffin. I thought this one was from Peter.

When I lifted up the little flaps and opened the container, I got sicker than I've ever been without vomiting. The container was stuffed with a messy, slimy, and very dead bird. The head was partially torn off and the whole container was alive with fat, little white worms. I had a real sicko in my world, one who was probably watching my revolted reaction to the gift with pleasure.

I said to myself, "You don't have time to think about what kind of monster could send you this kind of message, Amy! Just find the killer before the killer finds you."

I knew this had been a strong warning and I suspected the next one could be even fatal. Well, I wasn't one to panic. Having said that, I felt my knees buckle under me so I was forced to sit down. I was scared to death, damn it.

I recovered and went to the production department and found a box. I carefully put the container inside, trying to touch it as little as possible. I'd read enough murder mysteries to know all about fingerprints. Unfortunately, most people who read did too and so do all clever murderers. The police would have to be really lucky to find a print.

When Joe came over tonight I wouldn't be waiting with a cool drink or a delicious snack like other girls might. I'd just give him the bird.

# Chapter Twenty-Three

It was going on towards five o'clock and I was exhausted. Detecting can be brutal, let me tell you. Also, in addition to my Herculean efforts at detection, I had even managed to get a small amount of work done for the agency. Time to go home.

The sad thing was, at the end of the day, I had no idea, not a glimmer, of who had acted the guiltiest of my first three suspects. They all had gone ape, even Hy Voss in his quiet, chilling way. I was afraid I might have to forget the whole thing and leave detecting to Joe.

What nonsense, I thought, brightening up. So what if the first round of lies hadn't flushed anyone out? I would just have to come up with bigger and better lies for tomorrow. As exaggeration and truth twisting are talents that every good ad writer should have, I hoped that after a good night's sleep, I would be able to think of hundreds.

That idea cheered me up so much that I started daydreaming lies, mulling them over as I headed for the elevator. This was probably why I didn't see Mary Dee coming at me. The first thing that registered was another large mug of very hot coffee thrown all over me. It hurt, I screamed, and Mary Dee laughed.

"So, so sorry, Amy," she purred, "Did it leave a huge blister that hopefully will turn into an ugly scar?"

"Your concern touches me deeply but there's no blister, no scar. I didn't feel a thing besides a little wet."

"Oh, what a shame. Of course you realize it was just an unfortunate accident. I meant it to go right in your face and I missed. Just consider this my practice run."

"Call it anything you like. I call it a guilty person's big mistake. Trying to harm me is an act that makes you look desperately guilty. I can almost hear the clanging of the jail door closing on you as you start your new career as a felon. That's a job for which you have real talent, unlike the creative work you're so lousy at now."

Snarling, she started for me, but I ran for the elevator. Luckily, the elevator arrived before Mary Dee could get to me and it was full of people. I hustled in and the doors shut in her face. I pushed the button for garage and got my usual thrilling jolt as the high-speed elevator rocketed down forty-seven floors. We stopped at the main floor and all the other passengers got out.

When I got out in the garage, I was alone, so I was very careful to stop and look around. My meeting with Mary Dee had been uncomfortable. Meeting another of the suspects in this huge, dim and empty garage would be not very much fun, either.

I didn't see a soul, so I headed for my car. As I got closer, a man stood up, his back towards me. He'd been looking at my car. I couldn't decide whether to try and make it back to the elevator or just stop where I was and hope someone else would come.

Then he turned and saw me and smiled his handsome, sexy smile. It was Geno Pirelli. I relaxed a little.

"Amy, doll, I'm glad I caught you before you got scared."

"Too late," I quavered. "I already am."

"Sorry. No, I meant scared when you got to your car and saw the damage. Someone else got there first. And I'm afraid it's someone who doesn't think you're the cutest little thing on order, like I do. Well, usually you're a looker. But what have you been pouring all over yourself today?"

"Its just coffee. Never mind. Tell me about the damage. Has something happened to my car?"

"Just come on over here and see for yourself. Someone must have tried to puncture every single one of your tires. That probably was taking too long so they ended up slashing them. They're ruined. You got yourself an enemy, sweet hips?"

I don't know what made me sicker, the loss of all four, not-even-bald, tires or Geno's smarmy, pseudo-sexy way of talking to women. I didn't say anything.

Geno oiled on. "Now, honey, don't you fret. Geno is gonna give you a ride in his nice, new Porche. I'm going to take you home. You wait until I run upstairs and drop off this corrected copy."

As always, someone messing with my copy made me forget everything else. Who did he think he was? He was a writer just because his mother owned the company? Disgusting. I gritted my teeth and said, "And what did you think was the matter with my copy?"

"I just tweaked it a tiny bit, sweetie pie, otherwise Mama doesn't think I'm working hard enough. I need to have a little input."

"No you don't. Hiring a professional to do a job and then doing it yourself is like getting a dog and then barking yourself. Waste of time, talent and money. Not too smart."

"Cute little Amy. Did anyone ever tell you that you aren't wonderfully tactful at dealing with a client?"

Actually, after one painful incident, it had been strongly suggested, with some heat to back it up, that I never again go near clients, let alone talk to them. And Geno was our biggest client. So I shut up and just looked at him.

I noticed something funny. The knees on his expensive pants were filthy. He hadn't been just bending over to look at my tires. He'd been down on his hands and knees. Geno, my possible murderer number three, must have been doing more than just looking at my car.

"Sorry, Geno," I said in a very little voice, "I didn't mean to make you angry. Feel free to do whatever you want to the copy even though it ruins it."

"I'm not angry. How could I be with a sweet thing like you? So you just sit tight a minute. I'll open the Porsche and you can wait there while I go upstairs."

My voice was shaking as I said, "I'd love to, but I can't. I have an appointment with the sheriff from Bayfield. He's waiting for me now and he'll come looking for me if I don't show up soon."

"Sugar, you're breaking my heart. Isn't there a way you and I can get together tonight? I can promise you that you'll enjoy me, or rather, my company."

"Maybe we can get together tomorrow at the agency. I have some information that's important and that you should know. It involves you and it's about the murders."

I glanced at Geno as I said this and saw a transformation as great as though he'd donned a mask. The expensively styled black curls, the perfect Roman profile, the hot body were all still in evidence. But the lazy charm disappeared from his eyes and his lips thinned to a slit. He looked every inch a descendent of his Mafia relatives. He looked like a man who could kill and enjoy it.

"I knew you'd pushed your way into the murder investigations, Amy. That's a very poor hobby for such a defenseless little thing. But please, tell me what you know. I'm curious."

"I don't really know anything, Geno, honest. I did overhear one of the police make a remark about you and Stephano. Seems someone saw you having a very big argument with him Saturday evening."

Geno reached over a grabbed my upper arm so tight it hurt. "And just what was this argument about?"

"They didn't know. They said you were talking in Italian."

"I suppose conversing in a foreign language is enough to make one look guilty to those flatfoots. Who was the eavesdropper?"

"They didn't say. I don't know anything more. I don't. I just thought I should tell you what I'd overheard. I wanted to do you a favor."

"And just why would you want to do me a favor?"

I prayed for a really believable lie and said, "I've always had fantasies about you, Geno. All the women in the agency think you're molto good-looking and charming. I'd like to get to know you better."

"That's funny, honey. I recall putting the moves on you more than once and you ripped me up good. You had no interest in playing with me at all."

"I was just playing hard to get," I said, fluttering my eyelashes so hard I almost lifted off. "Plus I was engaged at the time so it would have been wrong of me, a mortal sin almost, to have encouraged you."

Geno's face relaxed just enough so that I knew my end was not going to be today. But he still looked grim, and he reached over and pushed his finger right into my chest.

He said very quietly, "Better watch it, Amy. Whoever slashed your tires has a very sharp knife. Sharp enough to push through here and slide right into your heart."

With that he turned away and left. He left me with queen-sized jitters and a strong inclination to drop my life in criminal investigation and get on the first plane to London. That would avert two tragedies. First, it would stop my darling Ryan from dating anyone else. Second, I wouldn't get killed.

As I stood by my car, staring at my ruined tires and wondering how in hell I was going to get home, two black-and-white Minneapolis squad cars rolled in. Out of the first, like an answer to the proverbial maiden's prayer, jumped Joe Bear.

He smiled and seemed really glad to see me until he noticed the flat tires. Then he proceeded to get very loud and mean. A long, public humiliation ensued during which he accused me of playing with my life and almost asking to be murdered plus getting into and probably ruining what was police business. His business. He didn't say which he thought was worse—my danger or my buttinsky ways.

I drew myself up to a full five-foot-three plus and said, "Just one moment, Sheriff. Do you have a shred of proof that I've been interfering in your case? And by the way, funny it's become *your* case, singular, now that you think you don't need me anymore."

"Cut the crap, Amy. I know you and I know you've been messing in things you shouldn't. I assume you must want to die. People don't slash the tires of women they like. Just the ones who meddle. You've had your busy, little fingers in every evil plot you could dream up. I'll bet you tried something with every person you think might be a suspect. Who threw coffee all over you, for example?"

I sniffed haughtily. "Really that is absolutely none of your business. It was an accident. But if I had been interfering, as you put it, I would have been doing you a favor. Someone has to keep the heat on. You weren't even around today. Nothing was being done."

A tiny little groan and some nasty mutters came next before Joe said, "You're wrong, but I'm not going to argue with you. To keep you safe, I'm going to have to jail you, aren't I?"

"Of course not. I'm all done trying to help you. Let the murderer go free. I wash my hands of it. I will be spending my free time meeting and then dating new, interesting, good-looking and sympathetic men."

Joe laughed in spite of himself. Then he called over to Deputy Mike, who actually looked glad to see me, and said to him, "I want you to stay with Ms. Connolly until the crime squad comes to go over this car. Then call and have her garage come and get it and take it in to get new tires. Do you have AAA, Amy?"

"Yes, but no money for tires. They should call me before they put anything on. I'll have to wait for some insurance money."

"Okay. Mike, after the car goes, take Ms. Connolly home. Stay with her until I get there tonight."

Deputy Mike said, "Okay Joe, but can you get her to promise not to try and lose me? I don't know the city all that well and I don't want to feel responsible if she gets away and killed. I like her."

I liked Deputy Mike too, and I didn't want to be killed either, so I promised and I really meant it.

Joe continued, "You drive me so crazy nuts that I forgot what I wanted to tell you. I was bringing you good news. Angela is not now nor has she ever been missing."

"Oh, thank God. Where is she? Why did she leave without calling me?"

"She's home in her own apartment. She came back to the Cities yesterday afternoon. I don't know who she called."

"Did she ask to see me? No? Well, I've got to see her right away. She'll relax when she's with me and then she'll remember who the murderer is."

"Oh, good. Then you and Angela can both be in danger and get killed together. This is not going to happen. You are going home and staying there under guard. Do I make myself clear?"

I didn't answer so Joe turned to Deputy Mike and said, "I'm handing you the most onerous of all duties, guarding a person who thinks she's invincible. My advice? Ignore her, just go to her apartment and stay there. Don't listen to any of her talk. Just sit on her until I get there."

"I'll do my best Joe," Mike said nervously.

Joe continued, "Amy I need to hear what you know before I leave. I want to find out just what lie you tried on which people. Let's move out of earshot for a minute. I've had a call from Hy Voss's lawyers. What in God's name did you do to him?"

"I told him a little lie. Actually two lies. One was a little one, the other was a humdinger."

"Why did you think it was a keen idea to lie to a murder suspect? This is supposing you don't actually have a death wish."

"It wasn't that big a deal. I just tried to wake up some sleeping bears to see what might come roaring out."

"Did you learn anything worth betting your sweet little ass for?"

"Don't be vulgar. Of course, I learned something. Mac, Mary Dee, Hy and Geno could all be guilty. They all got very upset with my harmless little lies and an innocent person wouldn't. And each one of the four threatened me. It wasn't a lot of fun. It was pretty awful actually."

Joe gave me a smile and patted my arm, "So tell me the threats."

"Hy said if I continued with my meddling, I would be murdered for sure."

"That was scary. We'll be talking to him about that."

"That wasn't even the meanest thing he said. Next he told his secretary to call payroll and dock my pay."

"In your financial spot and needing those tires, I can see how that hurt. How about Mary Dee?"

"Mary Dee threw a very heavy pot full of coffee at me and if I hadn't ducked I would have hit my head and we wouldn't be having this conversation or any conversation ever again. Just now Geno told me that whoever had slashed my tires has a very sharp knife, one that could be easily pushed right through me into my heart."

"You've had a bad day, Amy. I could almost feel sorry for you. You did bring it on yourself, but the results were way too dramatic. They all do sound guilty. How about number four, your old boyfriend Mac?"

"Don't insult me. Mac was never my boyfriend. I only went out with him to avoid staying home when every other possible friend was out of town or busy. And, Mac did threaten me. He actually said that I was no longer a candidate to become Mrs. Mac Larson."

"Oh, poor Amy. That must have stung. Getting old, without a firm offer of marriage in sight must frighten you."

I gnashed my teeth but went on, "He did threaten me too. He was screaming at me to get out. And you should have seen his face. He looked like he hated me."

Joe reached over and hugged me. "It wasn't fun at all being a detective today, was it, honey? You were scared, and I wasn't here. I'll try my best not to let that happen again."

I looked at Joe. He was so sweet and understanding. I felt myself once more liking him with a little dose of lust thrown in. I said, "But how you can promise me that, Joe? You're so busy."

"Simple. You're now in Police Custody. Explain that to her, Mike. And Mike, you have my permission to put the cuffs on her if necessary."

With that Joe was gone and I realized again how awful and tacky and unfair and pig-headed he was, and how much I disliked him.

I had to get free of poor Deputy Mike so I could get back into business and solve these murders. I certainly didn't need Joe to help me. This was a man with fatal flaws — total arrogance and a misplaced sense of humor.

# CHAPTER TWENTY-FOUR

I DO EXAGGERATE A TAD OCCASIONALLY but it really felt like it took three years to get my car taken care of. Cars bored me. This was probably because I'd never had a car I really loved or picked out myself. I got my brothers' hand-me-downs. This one was from my priest brother and a more yawn-inducing car had never rolled off an assembly line. It was an elderly beige sedan with a stick shift and no air. His grateful parishioners gave him a newer car for Christmas. His new car was gray, already second-hand, and, when it got older, I'd be driving it. And be damned glad to get it.

Deputy Mike said hopefully, "Time to go home, Amy. You're probably tired. I know I am."

"Absolutely, Mike. Straight home right after we stop briefly at Angela's."

"Wait a minute. Joe didn't say anything about stopping anywhere."

"You must have missed it. He said something on his way out. I know he wants me to try and get a little more information from her. He was very strict about it though. He said he'd let me see Angela but just for ten minutes. And he added that you had to be with me every one of those minutes."

"I guess that'll be okay then. Ten minutes."

"That's all, Mike. And it's on the way home."

Hell hovered closer with each lie. Lying to this good man was so easy and so wrong. But I figured the Lord would cut me a deal if I helped bring a murderer to justice.

We pulled up in front of Angela's apartment and I noticed her car was out in front of the building. I would have to tell her that I didn't think this was such a swell idea with a murderer around who had already tried to do her in. A madman might plant a bomb in it or something. Angela should keep her car out of sight and safe in the underground parking stall that came with her unit. Honestly, some women don't know how to stay safe in the city.

A man was coming out of the building as Deputy Mike and I got to the door so we just slipped in without having to call Angela's apartment for her to let us in. People aren't supposed to let strangers in but I imagine the sight of Mike in his full sheriff's uniform was pretty reassuring. We took the elevator to the third floor and rang Angela's doorbell. Nothing happened. I knew she had to be home with her car out in front like that. So I just leaned on the bell, and I could hear the buzz echo all up and down the hall. Finally we could hear steps coming to the door.

When the door opened, Angela was looking pretty bad. Her hair was all mussed up and flying around. She had a robe on and it looked like not much else underneath.

She didn't sound happy either as she said, "Amy, what are you doing here? Why didn't you call?"

"I wanted to surprise you and I knew you'd be glad to see me. I have lots to tell you."

"Well, I'm not able to see you right now. I'm sorry but I'm busy."

"You have company?" I was shocked. It was so unlike lonely, little Angela.

She put her hand to her mouth in a shushing way. "Please. I don't want to discuss my life with all my neighbors."

"Who is it? Someone new? I didn't know you were seeing anyone."

"I'm not really. It's a boy from home, from New Prague. He used to have a big crush on me when I was beautiful and now, well, now I get lonely. And he gets lucky."

"So he's the one that gave you a ride back to the Cities?

"Right."

"And that's why your car is out in front. His is in the garage."

"Yes. Could we take this up later? I told you, Amy, I really can't talk right now. If you'd called from the lobby, I wouldn't have answered the phone. You were making such a racket I knew I had to answer the door. If the neighbors saw the policeman with you, they'd all come out demanding to know what was going on. I don't want to get to know them. They already think I'm a freak."

"Sorry, Angela. We'll go. But first I'd like to tell you about my plan for catching the person who hurt you."

Angela ran her hands through her long blond hair and said heavily, "Leave it alone, Amy. Leave things alone, please. You're going to get hurt yourself. Or killed. I'll be in to work tomorrow. We can talk then."

She started to close the door and gave me a sad little wave goodbye as she did.

I had expected praise and glory. This had been a real cold water dunk. The only thing she didn't do to make me feel unwelcome was to set her cat on me. I wondered if she knew that I had saved her life. Maybe no one had told her what a hero I was.

If they had, she certainly would have acted more grateful. As always, my feelings soon changed. My pity for Angela always overcame any annoyance I felt for her no matter how she acted.

I was pretty sure I was her only friend. I would always forgive her. She'd had such a terrible life and mine had been so lucky. I was even glad about the high school boyfriend. It was nice that she'd found someone to be close to even though he might only be taking advantage of her loneliness. *I'll bet he's married*, I said to myself.

"C'mon Mike," I said cheerfully. "Let's go home. That is unless you want to stop and have a pizza on the way. There's nothing to eat in my kitchen. Nothing."

Mike did not think it was a good idea to stop at a restaurant. He was already nervous in case Joe had called and found us not at home where we should be. We compromised and stopped just long enough at Papa Murphy's to get my favorite pizza, the kind with everything on it, and then a stop at Kitty Korral to pick up my cat.

It was so great to be back in my little apartment. It was in a wonderful old Kenwood mansion that a good architect made over into six teeny apartments. I had one large room, a combination living room, kitchen and dining room, plus a very small bedroom and a bath. It was on the third floor so I got exercise in spite of my natural sloth. My parents refused to come to my place more that a couple times a year. They arrived out of breath and spent the next hour griping about the non-comfort of my old and droopy chairs. I thought my décor and furniture were sharp, really in. I found most of by just cruising the Kenwood alleys. These rich old-money people in Kenwood would throw out anything.

My apartment had a small balcony that Basil, my gorgeous, spoiled and temperamental cat, loved. He'd sit out there for hours making value judgments on passersby. He found my friends, and I suspect me, not quite up to his snuff.

The neighborhood was wonderful. It was about one block from Lake of the Isles where I could walk for three miles or just to the next available bench. I was so glad to be back. I loved my home. I opened the door and screamed.

Directly across the room from the door was a huge wreath on a stand in front of the fireplace. It looked to be almost as tall as I was and was made from dark green, glossy leaves and dark purple flowers. There was a black satin banner across the front of the wreath with the words REST IN PEACE in gold.

Mike pushed me behind him, pulled out his gun and secured the apartment. There was no one there and nothing was disturbed unless you counted me. I was plenty disturbed.

Mike called Joe, and Joe promised that he would find out where the wreath had come from and how it had gotten into my apartment. In the meantime, he told Mike not to answer the door or let anyone in until he got there.

"Tell him I found the wrapping paper in the kitchen. The wreath is from Minneapolis Blooms," I hollered.

I was too skittish to sit still. I put all the shades down and turned off all the lights. I thought someone might take a shot at me through the windows. This was stupid considering I lived on the third floor. The killer would need a very long ladder. But I was scared. I put a blanket over the television, and Mike and I huddled under it and tried to watch a show.

I couldn't concentrate on even the dimmest of programs, one known to cause brain rot in three out of four viewers. My heart was still sliding around in my chest like I was on speed.

It kept erratic time while I wondered why I had gotten so deep into so much trouble and how I could squirm out. I knew I wouldn't be able to talk or beg my way out.

There was no way of going back and erasing what I'd started. I'd have to go on and finish solving the crimes before someone finished me. I was tired of fear. I craved action. By morning, I would have a foolproof plan and a partner I could count on. I sat and thought for a long time but no little light bulbs went off in my brain. Well, there were still hours until dawn.

The plan had to be perfect. No loose ends. I knew I would have to poke the suspects again, harder than before. The need for safety was paramount. The plan had to keep me at a distance. No more going into people's offices alone. No more getting thrown out or having things thrown on me. *Safety first*, I thought. I'd promised Joe not to get into trouble and I wouldn't. My new plan would be airtight. It would encase me completely in a bubble of security.

By nine o'clock I had a plan that could be carried out almost entirely long distance. I would send an invitation to each of the four suspects that they couldn't afford to ignore. I'd use one of the computers at work to send it to them via e-mail.

I would choose a place to meet where I'd be as safe as in a fortress. No matter how much the murderer might wish to harm me, if I chose a great spot he wouldn't be able to get close enough to ruffle my hair. I kept going over the plan again and again.

I finally knew that I had created the perfect sting operation. It was as good, I thought smugly, as any I'd ever seen in a movie or read in a mystery.

At ten o'clock the phone rang. Joe was in the lobby. I buzzed him up and checked him out before I cracked the door an inch. As soon as he was inside, I threw myself all over him and began to sob. Joe didn't pat me and say, "There, there," or "I told you so!" He just held me until I'd hiccupped my last hiccup and blown my nose. Then he told us what he'd found out.

"I'm afraid the florist didn't give us a name but we made some progress. I got one of the supervisors out of bed to come in and check out the orders. We did find both the order and the delivery slip. Minneapolis Blooms also keeps a tape of phone orders, which this was, and they found the tape and played it for us."

"Was it one of the people I think are our prime suspects? Did you recognize the voice at all?" I said.

"No I didn't. I'm pretty sure I've never heard that voice before. But we did get one clue from it. The caller was a woman."

"Aha! It had to be Mary Dee."

"I couldn't swear to that," Joe said regretfully.

I pressed on. "What about the charge slip?"

"The woman charged it to a Visa number so we got hold of Visa and checked that out. Brace yourself, Amy. The charge was on your Visa."

My panic abated as I seethed. Some low-crawling scum had the nerve to use my own money to terrify me.

"How did she get the wreath into my apartment?"

"She simply told the order writer at the florist to call your custodian and ask him to open your unit and put it in. She told him just to put it so you'd see it as soon as you opened the door. She said you were having a sort of after the funeral party for a relative tonight. He wasn't supposed to do that without orders from the owner. But he's fairly new and anxious to please."

"Well, what's next?"

"Nothing is next for you. Unless you want to sit down and plan your own funeral. You've had some strong warnings. The next step for the murderer will be physical harm or death. Yours."

"That isn't amusing, Joe."

"No one's laughing. I hope you're ready to listen to me. I have to go back down to the courthouse. We'll figure out a long-range plan for you in the morning. I want Mike to stay here with you tonight, go to work with you in the morning and stay right next to you, until I get there, probably tomorrow afternoon."

"I appreciate all you're doing to keep me breathing and I have every good intention to cooperate fully with the law."

I could tell that Joe didn't trust me, but I made my voice quaver and my eyes fill just slightly with tears. Those lessons at the Children's Theater when I as a kid were really paying off.

Joe sighed. "I hope you mean that. Mike, don't leave Amy alone unless she's in a meeting or conference with more than once person or leaves the door to offices open with you sitting right outside."

This was going to slow me down considerably but I nodded as though in perfect harmony with Joe. Why not be sweetly agreeable as long as I could?

# CHAPTER TWENTY-FIVE

In the morning, I was edgy but confident. I had come up with the perfect plan to catch a murderer with no risk to me. Deputy Mike drove me to work, and I tried to keep my nervousness from alerting him to my simmering excitement. We took the elevator to the Creative Department, and I scurried right into my own office. I sure didn't care to see any of the Big Four until tonight. Mike happily settled in at a desk outside my office. He trusted me, which made him such a sweet person and such a bad judge of character.

I opened my computer and took a look at my e-mail. There were some directions from account people about copy changes. As usual I ignored them. The suits loved to add turgid little bits of boring copy to everything.

There were also some letters. The first was a rabid handwritten letter from Mac. Next was an envelope with an old photo of me taken at an agency picnic last summer. Mary Dee had added splotches of what looked like blood all over the picture and signed her name in a big, bold type.

When I was done going through the mail, I went looking for Peter with Deputy Mike right behind me. I had decided that Peter would be my perfect back up. Now all I needed was to talk him into it. This would include solid sounding reasons why we must do this thing plus a boxcar full of encouragement to give Peter enough false hope in me to agree to be my second. If that didn't work, I'd use guilt. I was good at guilt.

"Hi, Peter. I have a job that we have to get down to right now."

"Forget it Amy. I'm in the middle of something great."

"Just let me tell you my ideas." I started talking like I was describing an ad campaign for Pirelli's new single-serving lasagna. "Let me show you what I mean. I need to use your computer to give you the flavor of the copy."

Actually, I needed to write to Peter so that Deputy Mike wouldn't know what I was doing. Peter was suspicious as hell because he had never heard of single-serving lasagna and suspected it was just a figment of my imagination. He complained bitterly but finally had to agree to let me show him my ideas. After Peter saved his work, I moved into his chair and started typing. I motioned to him to hang over my shoulder to read the screen as I typed to keep things private.

PETER: I NEED YOU TO COME WITH ME TONIGHT. I WILL BE MEETING THE MURDERER BUT I HAVE A VERY SAFE PLAN. I WILL NEED YOU TO HELP ME A TINY BIT BUT YOU WILL BE OUTSIDE IN YOUR CAR AND THERE IS NO CHANCE OF ANYTHING GOING WRONG OR OF YOU GETTING HURT.

Peter shook his head and said, "Amy, I don't like your ideas. I hate it when you work on things by yourself and then expect me to agree with them. I just can't get behind this campaign and that's final."

THEN I'LL HAVE TO GO ALONE AND I WILL. I CAN'T THINK OF ANYONE ELSE I TRUST LIKE I DO YOU. I'M INVITING FOUR SUSPECTS TO MEET ME TONIGHT IN THE PIRELLI KITCHENS. I FIGURE ONLY THE GUILTY ONE WILL SHOW UP. ALL I NEED YOU TO DO IS TO

WATCH FROM ACROSS THE STREET AND CALL 911 IF YOU SEE ANYTHING THE LEAST BIT QUESTIONABLE. COULDN'T BE EASIER OR SAFER. BUT IF YOU CAN'T FIND IT IN YOUR HEART TO HELP ME, I'LL GO BY MY- SELF EVEN THOUGH YOUR BACK-UP HELP WOULD KEEP ME SAFE.

Peter groaned, "I guess I'll have to." Then he pushed me out of the chair, leaned in and typed in a question for me. He wanted to know how I was planning to get rid of my police watchdog while I cruised around town after the murderer.

I typed in my response that included a rather mean trick I would have to play on poor Mike. I planned to make him a delicious nighttime drink and stick in half of a very mild sleeping pill I had left from the last overseas flight I'd been on. I swore to Peter that it was perfectly safe. I told him to pick me up at exactly 10:20 p.m. and we'd go over the fine points.

When I had finished, I turned off the computer and said to Peter, "I'm thrilled that you're going to work on this campaign with me. I know it'll turn out great, everyone's going to love it, and we'll be heroes. When have I ever led you astray?"

"Often," was his overly surly response. I ignored it and left his office before he changed his mind.

Next step was to find an empty office where I could create the invitation and send it out to the four suspects. I could use the one in the library or the media room but someone might come in and be too curious about what I was doing. I decided to go up to the top floor and look through offices of the junior executives. They were usually out of the office either at the clients, as they always claimed, or just goofing off, which was true most of the time. I found an office way in the back of the department, sat down and looked up the e-mail addresses of my four suspects. Then I typed the invitation:

I CAN'T TALK TO YOU IN THE OFFICE ANY-
MORE. PEOPLE ARE WATCHING. I KNOW WHAT
YOU DID. I DON'T WANT TO TURN YOU IN. BUT
I WILL NEED SOMETHING TO KEEP MY MOUTH
SHUT. WE CAN TALK ABOUT IT TONIGHT.
MEET ME IN THE PIRELLI PASTA KITCHENS AT
11:10. WE WILL HAVE 15 MINUTES TO COME TO
TERMS. COME ALONE.
A FRIEND

I typed in each e-mail address and sent the letters out one
at a time. My hands were ice cold and shaking when I was finished but all four of the letters were gone.

The chase was on.

# CHAPTER TWENTY-SIX

T HINGS STARTED GOING ASS-OVER-TEAKETTLE, as my grandma used to say, before I even left the house. First, Deputy Mike fell asleep before I could give him his delicious bedtime drink laced with half a sleeping pill. I couldn't be sure he'd stay asleep during my little foray so I had to wake him up to give it to him. Then I stood there and watched him while he drank it. I could tell he thought I was weirder than ever, but he drank it down like a lamb, to please me.

Peter caused the next unforeseen snag. He was on time but arrived driving a Beast, a rattletrap that belonged to Mark, his significant other.

"We can't take an old car to catch a murderer," I hissed. "Especially one that makes so much noise."

"I couldn't help it," Peter said defensively. "Mark needed my car tonight. He had to pick up a whole bunch of fresh vegetables for the restaurant. So it was either the Beast or nothing."

I was infuriated and said, "This plan was timed to run like a Swiss watch and you're gumming up the works. Do you want to get me killed?"

"Of course I don't want to get you killed. But if it comes to a choice, I choose Mark. You're crabby. Crabby and mean."

The ride was quite chilly after that, and I don't mean just the winter weather. We didn't really speak until we got to the main plant of Pirelli's Pasta. We found a spot where Peter could see the action clearly and where he would not be seen himself.

Pirelli's plant was actually several, large, connected buildings spread over two square blocks. The kitchens, where my
meeting was to take place, was on a very busy street. It had a
huge floor-to-ceiling glass window that allowed passersby to
watch the activity in the kitchens. The glass was one-way so
that onlookers had a great view but the home economists busy
working inside couldn't see them or be disturbed while working.

The window was perfect for my purpose. Peter could stay
hidden in my car but he would be able to see clearly every part
of where I was meeting the murderer.

Before I got out of the car and left Peter, I decided to make
up with him. After all, he was helping me and I could see he
was really nervous. I said generously, "Well, Peter, I forgive
you. This is a fine, fine thing you're doing. You're putting your
life right on the old line to avenge the murders of that poor
skier and Stephano and bring a little more justice into this
world."

"For God's sake, Amy, belt up. Things are black enough
without one of your Great Writer speeches. I'm sick now with
dread and I know this is the wrong thing to do. If you carry
on much longer, I'll pass out."

"Some people," I said stiffly as I climbed out of the car,
"some people don't know how to enjoy the drama of their own
lives."

"I don't know what that means, and I'll bet you don't either."

I ignored him. It was now 11:00 p.m. and there was no time
to spare. I went around the side of the building and in the em-
ployee entrance.

As I had planned, this entrance was very busy. One crew
had finished the shift and started to come out, as the new crew
came in. People glanced at me but no one stopped me. I had

dressed all in white, the color of the all-covering uniforms the staff wore. I think the crowds kept the guard's attention off me. I was just another worker coming on or going home.

I passed through the locker rooms where workers were changing clothes. The uniforms were white long pants, long-sleeved tops, hoods that covered the hair and a mask that covered the nose and mouth. When a worker was totally dressed, he or she looked like a giant white bunny. Between shifts, it was one enormous cage of bunnies. That gave me a funny feeling remembering the bunny that had tried to stab me on the fire road.

The next room was the enormous Prep Room and it was completely empty. My luck was holding. There was no one to stop me. The room had large covered plastic bins full of fresh onions, tomatoes, carrots, mushrooms, peppers, garlic, celery, and more. One table held large boxes of spices and cheese. The room was very cold to keep the vegetables fresh and safe. I didn't linger though; the staff would be coming soon. I hurried through to the cooking room. I intended to wait there for two minutes until 11:05 p.m. when I would go next door to the Kitchens and get ready to meet a murderer.

This was the largest room of all. It held the giant mixers and cookers that made the pasta and pizza sauces. The cooking pots were enormous and there were nearly a dozen of them. Each was about seven feet in diameter and about six feet deep. Each cooker was set into the floor with part of the cooker on the floor below where each has a stove beneath it. Each cooker was about four feet deep on this floor with two feet on the floor below. All the cookers seemed to be running so they must have all been full. It was an absolutely awesome sight.

It was dark there, empty and quiet between work crews. I could hear the plop, swish of the mixers. I noticed that a cover had been left off one cooker. That was funny. They were usually very careful to keep things sterile. Maybe it was empty. I walked over to the kettle and looked in. It was full of a red mess that looked like sticky blood.

I was grateful I had just a minute or more to wait and then I'd go into the test Kitchen where Peter could see me. I wasn't really nervous though. I wasn't like one of those dumb women in slasher movies who were always walking right into traps. I had been careful to bring a back up.

I heard something and turned around to look. No one. I turned back and found myself staring at a big white rabbit. I circled around the kettle, keeping my distance. When he moved, I moved, always keeping half the cooker between us. I was still okay and I knew someone must come in soon. I was so intent on keeping away from him that I didn't notice there was a second white rabbit behind me. Not only was this guy a murderer, he was also a big cheat. He'd come early and he hadn't come alone.

Before I could say anything, the second rabbit grabbed my arms and spun me around. He pushed me into the kettle so hard that it took the breath out of me. I tried to turn my head enough to see who it was but all I could see was white. White clean-room suit, white hat, and white mask.

He started pushing me up, trying to shove me over the side of the kettle. I kicked back hard, trying to get him somewhere that would really hurt. He grabbed my leg instead and had an even greater hold on me. *Oh, God*, I thought, *I'm going to go in that kettle*. I couldn't get hold of anything. The stainless steel sides of the kettle were too slippery. And my legs were too damn short. I was kicking and screaming but I was going over. I was sliding down. I was falling. But I still had my hands on the rim.

Not for long. I felt myself lifted up and thrown in. And then one of them was behind me and was pushing my head under the sauce. They were going to drown me.

I couldn't see. I couldn't breathe. My nose was plugged. Big, whole tomatoes were bumping against my closed eyes. I was trying to keep my nose and mouth closed, but I wanted to scream. I was panicking. I thought, *I'm going to drown in tomato sauce.*

The ridiculous horror of it struck me. I was to be the butt of a macabre farce. The way I would die would be a big joke to a lot of people. That stiffened my spine and I thought, no, I would not drown without a fight. I figured I had enough breath and strength left for one big push out. But I didn't know which way was out. If I had kicked down instead of up, I would be out of air. I gave up again and started sinking. Then I felt a little heat under my feet, from the burners below. They must have just turned them on. That little hint of warmth told me up was the other way. I kicked out and felt some movement through the sticky mess. I tried to go straight up and away from the bottom. I had no breath left. I gave one last despairing push, a lunge toward the top.

I burst out of the sauce. I could feel cool air on my arms, then my face. I had my head out, and I wiped my face and took a breath like gold, like love, a breath that was life.

The white rabbits were gone and a loud siren blast filled the air. Almost a single breath later, the room was full of men in uniforms. I yelled but no one heard me through the noise of the siren. I tried to hang on to the sides but they were even slipperier because I was coated with sauce. I had to float with my head out of the sauce until someone noticed me. Finally, two officers saw me, got hold of my arms and dragged me out of the kettle.

I lay on the floor like a small, beached whale while they tried to question me. When I could talk, I asked, "Did you get them?"

"Get who?" one of the officers said.

"The rabbits. The two big white rabbits. They were going to kill me."

They thought I was hallucinating but I finally yelled loud enough to get them to understand me. I asked them to call the Hennepin County Sheriff's Office and get Joe Bear down here. He'd be able to get them to start really looking. They agreed. Most of the police force spread out to look for the two workers.

"Look for the ones with tomato sauce all over their sleeves," I said.

The two who stayed with me began cordoning off the area.

The noise stopped. Someone had finally turned off the siren. Suddenly the doors to the room were filled with a lot of big white rabbits. The new crew was waiting to come in. They saw the cover off and the mess and I heard one of them say the kettle would have to be emptied and sterilized. I screamed, "Don't touch that kettle. There could be fingerprints."

They edged away. I don't know if they stopped because they believed me or because I looked so crazy. The two police who had stayed with me decided it was time to question me.

I asked, "How did you know I was in trouble?"

"We didn't. They were just answering a burglary call. When the siren went off, it also tripped an alarm at the closest police precinct."

"Who turned in the alarm?"

"Your friend did. He says when you didn't show up in the kitchen window, he knew you were in trouble and there wasn't time to get help. So he got out your tire jack and threw it through the front door. It set off the alarm and we came running. You're lucky it was an old, heavy jack. The new ones couldn't have broken that door."

I felt a rush of gratitude and love flood over me for Peter. What a true, blue, clever pal. I would do anything, anything in the world for him. I would let him have the last word on our joint creative approaches without an argument for a whole year. Well, for a month anyway.

I asked the police if I could go into the women's locker room and take a shower and they agreed. I'd clean up fast and be ready when Joe finally got here. I picked out a white uniform to wear home.

It was good to slip out of my soggy clothes and pick the big pieces of tomato out of my hair. I never appreciated the healing powers of a warm shower until that night.

## Chapter Twenty-Seven

My HEAD AND FACE WERE FULL OF SHAMPOO when I head the sound of the outer door opening and then footsteps coming closer. I was trying to wipe off as much shampoo from my face and eyes as I could when the door of the shower crashed open and smashed onto the far wall. I was so terrified I was afraid I was going to quit breathing. Dear God, I thought, this is like that scene from Psycho. And tonight I was to be the victim.

A voice said, "He's gone and he's never coming back, and it's your fault. It's all been your fault, you nosy, stinking bitch."

I thought I knew the voice but I wasn't sure and my eyes were still full of soap so I couldn't see clearly. I said, "Who are you? And who's gone?"

"You know who's gone you conniving piece of dog shit. My beautiful lover is gone and he's never going to come back."

She threw me a towel and said, "Don't try anything, I have a gun. But wipe your eyes. I want you to see me as I kill you."

"Angela? Angela!!"

"Surprised? If you were one half as smart as you think you are, you would have guessed long ago."

"Angela, listen to me. I'm your friend. Your good friend."

Her face contorted in fury. "You're not my friend. It made you feel powerful to be nice to me. You were so condescending, so full of good advice on how to be happy. Oh, my God, how I've hated you."

I prayed for something that might soften her or at least stop her until help came.

I said, "But we did things together, spent time and had fun. You must have some good feelings for me."

"You were just a little bit better than nothing. You and my grandparents were all I had."

"I was kind to you. You can't say I wasn't kind."

"That was the worst, your pity. You actually felt sorry for me. Who in the hell do you think you are? You're a short, average looking, freckled nothing most men would pass by without a look. I was beautiful, one of the most beautiful women in the world. Your talking down to me used to make me laugh until I hated you enough to kill you."

"Feeling sorry for you is such a terrible thing? So terrible that I have to die?"

"All of this, everything is your fault. That's why Geno had to leave me. I was to hold your head under the sauce until you died. He left to go and get the car. You struggled so long that I was late getting there, and Geno had to leave without me."

"Angela, he double-crossed you. He left you to take the blame."

"No, that's not true. Geno loves me."

"If he'd loved you, he would have waited."

"Shut your filthy, lying mouth. If you hadn't interfered I could have taken care of Mary Dee and none of the rest of this would have happened. And you might have lived because Geno and I would be gone."

"You killed the girl on the ski hill?"

"That was your fault. You made me kill her. First you put on Mary Dee's bib number so when I shot at you I thought it was her. Then you fell down right as I shot and instead of killing you, the bullet killed that stranger."

"Why didn't Geno do his own dirty work?"

"You're so stupid. Everyone knew Geno was like catnip to that alley cat Mary Dee, who was blackmailing him. The cops would find out and suspect him. He had to have a perfect alibi for the time of the murder. You almost ruined it when you showed up on the road Geno was using to get on the trail, after leaving the gun for me."

"He tried to kill me."

"He thought you were Mary Dee. Geno didn't kill anyone."

"No he turned you into a killer, one without an alibi. Angela, he used you."

"You don't know crap. Geno thought up a perfect alibi for me. He'd just give me a little tap on the head, leave me in the chair lift and you'd all think I was a victim."

"Angela, Geno double-crossed you twice. First he hit you so hard you had a severe concussion that almost killed you. When that didn't work, he packed you in snow and left you out there to die."

"That was your fault. You told me you would come looking for me if I didn't show up downstairs in thirty minutes. That gave us just enough time to set the scene outdoors. But you didn't come looking in thirty minutes. You forgot all about me for nearly an hour. You left me on the ski hill to die. But I didn't die. And now you will."

I had to get through to her somehow. I took a deep breath and said, "No, Angela, I'm the one who found you. Didn't they tell you? I looked for your car. I called the police. I'm the one who noticed that the chairs were running on the ski hill."

"Too late, you were too late. If you'd come on time, Stephano wouldn't have been sneaking around and seen us. Then he had to die. That was your fault too."

"You can stop this killing now, Angela. And I'll help you. I can get my brother Fitz to represent you. You know he's the best trial lawyer in town."

"Still looking down your piggy little nose, thinking of how you can fix me? You're so damn predictable with your goody-two-shoes ideas for making things nice. I don't want to be fixed. I've lost Geno. My life is over. So yours must be over too."

"Please, Angela, hear me. Don't give up your life for Geno. He doesn't deserve it. He double-crossed you and left you here to face the blame."

"You sexless hag. You don't understand real passion. Geno loves me. He thought I was beautiful. He said he never saw my scars or funny face when he looked at me. He saw me always the way I used to be. He was going to marry me right after I killed Mary Dee and he divorced his wife."

"Oh, Angela you can't believe that."

"Shut up, shut up. It's over now. If I didn't hate you so much, I'd ask you where you want the bullet — heart or head. But there's not going to be an easy death for you. I'm going to shoot you in the stomach. They say it's the most painful death of all and it will take you a long time to die."

I was looking at Angela, but behind her I saw the door to the room open a sliver slowly and silently. I said quickly, "Please give me just a moment or two to say my prayers, make my act of contrition. Please, I'm begging you."

"I knew you'd beg, you sniveling coward. You have fifteen seconds."

The door opened a bit more. It was Joe. I had been holding the towel Angela had given me behind my back. The water was still running and the towel had become quite heavy. If I could swing it out before she shot, I might have a chance. The door opened a little wider and made a tiny noise. Angela turned just a hair toward the noise and I swung the towel out as hard as I could. It hit her right in the face and knocked her to her knees. She scrambled to get back in position but Joe was faster. He slammed Angela down and got the gun and cuffed her. It was over.

Joe called for reinforcements, but the fight was gone from Angela. She lay on the floor, repeating over and over, "It was all her fault. She made me do it. He loves me. He would never double-cross me. It was her fault, her fault."

Joe threw me a big, dry towel and I sat down on the floor of the shower and wept. After the Minneapolis police came and took Angela away, Joe pulled me up and wrapped the towel around me. Then he just held me tight until my sobs stopped. I said, "Joe, Joe get Geno. It was Geno's plan, all of it. He talked Angela into killing for him."

"I've been pretty sure it was Geno since Sunday. But I didn't have enough proof and I never suspected Angela's involvement."

I said, "I thought it was Mary Dee. Well, I wanted it to be. But I think Mary Dee's been terrified since Saturday. I should have known that meant she wasn't guilty. So are you going after Geno?"

"We have an all points bulletin out for him, but I don't think we're going to get him tonight. I think he's gone beyond our law."

"Where is he?"

"If I'm right, he's on his way to Sicily. His mother left in her private jet about an hour after the alarm went off here. We've contacted Interpol. The Italian police will meet Mama's plane. But Geno probably won't be on it. The Italian police think they'll have touched down somewhere else and dropped Geno off before landing in Palermo."

"Leaving Angela to take all the blame. But why would Mama Pirelli take a risk like this? She was always complaining about Geno. She thought he was lazy, selfish and just like her husband who everyone said she hated."

"Ah, Amy, that is *famiglia*. Mama is Geno's mother. And he's all she's got."

"Do you mean to say, that she can keep him hidden for-ever? That he'll never be brought to justice?"

"I think it's possible. But don't worry. Geno will be pun-ished. He was given a life sentence. He will never be able to leave Sicily as long as he lives. This might be a short life be-cause his wife and her relatives, the Antonnucis, live there and they'll be looking for him."

# CHAPTER TWENTY-EIGHT

AFTER THAT, I GOT DRESSED, and Joe took me home. It was almost 2:00 a.m. He asked Deputy Mike to stay with me for the rest of the night. I was still in shock, but I was so tired I went right to sleep but had recurring nightmares all night long. I was definitely done with sticking my nose into murder.

When I woke up the next morning, I was as tired as I'd ever been in my life. The sun was shining, though, the murdering was over and I felt strangely peaceful. When I came out of the bedroom, Mike had the coffee ready. I asked him for the morning papers and he looked kind of funny. "The papers aren't here yet, Amy."

"Neither the *Minneapolis Tribune* or the *St.Paul Pioneer Press*? What a bummer. I wonder if Angela's arrest is in the paper?"

Mike shook his head, so I went over and turned on the television. They had just finished the national and state news and local items were next. Up came a ghastly picture. It was me, slumped against the kettle in the Pirelli plant, and covered in sauce with whole pieces of tomato in my hair. The two buffoon announcers hee-hawed their way through the story of the murder attempt with little jolly asides like "Boy, she really looks sauced, doesn't she?"

Worse, someone had given them my name and they promptly told everyone in our five-state area. I would have another five minutes of dubious, embarrassing fame.

"Give me the papers, Mike," I said. "I know you just hid them to spare my feelings."

Mike dug them out, and I looked with horror at both front pages. There I was again. It's criminal that any idiot with a cell phone can take pictures of you without your consent and make a lot of money from the media. I couldn't remember anyone there last night using their phone but it had happened. Here was the ugly proof.

Joe arrived before long and said, "Geno has gotten away. His mother's in Sicily and claims she has no idea where he is, but she knows he's innocent. She swears to clear his good name if it costs her every penny. She has a lot of pennies. She just might be able to do it."

All my good work was for nothing? Angela was in custody, but Joe told me that she had gone into a psychotic state and they were going to hospitalize her instead of jailing her for the present. I asked, "She will be locked up, really tight?"

"Really, really tight. She's more of a threat to herself now than anyone else. You have nothing to worry about. I came to tell you that and to say goodbye before I take off for Hayward. I'm going to finish the paper work up there where most of the action took place. And I've got to get going on my campaign. I'm running for the Wisconsin legislature from Bayfield County. I've got my committee to set up, speeches to write, money to raise and ads to prepare."

"That's something I could help you with. I could come up next weekend and get started."

"Ah, Amy, not for a while. I'm eager for you and me to spend a lot of time together but not during the campaign. If I thought voters would believe that we are just platonic friends, I'd say come ahead. But my feelings for you are lots hotter than that, so we'll have to put things on a back burner until after the votes are in."

I had to agree that I probably wouldn't be an asset to a single guy running for office. I was disappointed though. Joe had just stopped cold our growing friendship, or whatever it was, for now. I did have the satisfaction of knowing that he was somewhat interested, just not enough to take a chance with his political career.

My self-confidence was in shreds. No matter how nicely stated, the truth was two guys had dumped me in two days. Probably a new record.

I told myself I was glad it was Saturday and I'd have the weekend to get ready for work Monday. I had lots to catch up on today. After I picked up my stopped mail and shopped for groceries, I came back to the apartment and gave it a good cleaning. Then I ran out of things I had to do except for dodging Basil. He was hiding under my bed and taking swipes at me as I walked by. He was furious with me for leaving him at Kittty Korral. Basil had always hated cats.

Except for my hissing cat, the apartment was mighty quiet and very depressing. There were no phone messages. Joe had gone to Bayfield, and Ryan had gone to London. There were no dates in sight. For the first time since I was fifteen years old, I was alone on Saturday night.

I picked up the phone and started calling my girlfriends. The first four were gone, out on dates, probably having a wonderful time. The fifth friend said she'd heard Ryan and I were split and would I mind if she went after him big time. I told her to go ahead and try, but it wouldn't be much use as Ryan had often told me how much he disliked her. Then I hung up and crossed her name off my phone list.

Sunday was the day I usually spent with my parents and the brothers. It came and it wasn't too bad. The brothers felt sorry for me. Mike said his fellow officers thought I was pretty brave. Father Kevin said he was sure God knew that my heart was in the right place. Fitz just rumpled my hair, called me Sprout, his pet name for me, and offered to sue anyone I wanted sued. My parents thought the picture and publicity were funny and my own fault.

It was all a ghastly letdown. Oh, well, I'd get the glory I deserved on Monday when I got to work. All the other suspects would be thrilled with me because I had cleared their names. And it wouldn't hurt the agency image any to have a real, live heroine writing copy there.

Monday dawned, ice cold of course, but with sunshine and a clear blue sky. I called a cab and I arrived at the agency early. As the day unfolded I must say it wasn't quite the triumph for me that I had expected. I went in first to see my boss, Chuck Pylon.

He told me that he talked to Virginia and told her everything. He said they'd had a rough weekend but that things were better than they had been with the secret between them. Chuck still seemed unhappy and nervous, but I just thought that was because of the trouble at home. I was wrong.

When I got to my office and opened my e-mail, the first one was one from Hy Voss. There was to be a meeting at 9:30 a.m. in the large conference room for the entire agency. So finally I was going to be publicly thanked.

Hy looked stuffy as ever as he announced, "This will impact every department. I am sorry to announce that we have lost one of our biggest clients. Pirelli Pasta called the media this morning to say they were dropping us and going with Leo Burnett. You all know this means changes. When the money goes, so do some of the jobs. If you will return to your departments, you'll learn what these changes are to be."

It turned out that three heads would have to roll in creative. One of those heads was mine, another was Peter's. The one bright and shining spot in the morning was that the third head to hit the floor was Mary Dee's.

So things hadn't gone quite the way I'd hoped and I wasn't too thrilled with being out of a job. But that's the way it was in advertising. The rule was usually last hired, first fired especially if you worked on the departing account. It was fair as these things go, and I knew I could find another job. Peter took it philosophically and said he wanted to keep working with me and that we should job-hunt together.

Softening the blow of being fired was Mary Dee's response. She shrieked, she wept, she threw things. It was wonderful. So getting canned wasn't all bad.

Plus, I might be a tad battered, but I was ever and always full of hope. I started looking for some silver linings to being unemployed. For example, I would now have time to go through junkyards for four not-too-bald tires.

Even better, I could take a vacation. I could fly to London and stay with Ryan. I knew he wanted me to come, we'd have a blast. I'd fend off the competition. Dreams of England in the spring with Ryan filled my head. I would go home and start to pack.

But how could I go to London? I was quite, quite broke. I was depressed for a moment until light dawned. I knew what to do. I knew where the blame lay.

I'd make the responsible parties pay. Everything bad that had happened to me was their fault. I'd get the money I needed for the trip from them. I'd sell those damn skis.

# More Than You Want to Know about the Author

Joan Murphy Pride graduated from the University of Minnesota in Journalism. She worked part time during college writing copy for Sears, Cook's Fashions, and Warner Hardware. After college, Joan wrote fashion copy for Powers and Dayton-Hudson. Following were stops in Twin Cities advertising agencies as copywriter. When her son was small, Joan opened a Creative Studio with Diane Syme. They produced all kinds of

advertising for agencies and directly for clients.

In a stunningly bad move, Joan next became CEO of Pride Barber & Pride, a full service agency with two men who wished she'd just shut up and make the coffee. Soon she was free-lance writing again and also published *Not So Fast* with Phebe Hanson. It's a funny memoir of a great, long trip to Europe. Currently, Joan is hard at work on a new Amy Connolly mystery called, for the nonce, *Another Bloody Opera*.

# Author's Note

The first Birkebeiner in the U.S. opened in Hayward, Wisconsin, in 1973 with one woman and thirty men skiers. Last year the Birkebeiner had 9,000 skiers. The race in this book is one early on. It was in the days when Telemark was the newest, posh resort with their own airstrip, the same fabulous cross-country trails plus down-hill skiing and lessons too.

My picture (opposite) is on one of those trails but never at a Birkebeiner. Look closely and you'll see the fear on my face, a poor skier out with great skiers—my darling Bob Pride, and Nancy and Dennis Rogers. I loved and trusted them, still do. But they always promised me the trail was easy and flat, and they always lied. And I always said I'd get even someday by writing a murder mystery where great skiers get killed and the beginner solves the murders.

# I'd Like to Thank . . .

Dennis Murphy Anderson, my son, who designed the cover, read the book four times, took me to meetings, readings, fixed my computer and more. Much more. He's the definitive perfect son.

My computer-savvy daughter-in-law, Stephanie, for doing magical things that keep me as organized as possible.

The Hartless Murderers--Jessie Chandler, Brian Landon, and T.J. Roth, my incredible, indispensable writing group. They do everything for me but write.

Kathleen Benson, Connie Nelson, Jean Liudahl, Rochelle Raming, and Bonnie Hiatt. You are the friends who were always there for me.

The dear friends and patient, intelligent, loving, mistake catching book readers: Phebe Hanson, Janet Donaldson, Rochelle Raming and Kathleen Benson.

The Bayfield Artists and writers who read the book two chapters a year: Mary Lou Child, Janet Donaldson, Alice Fjelstul, Lynne Fjelstul, Phebe Hanson, Elaine Haufman, Pratibha Gupta, Marion Mahoney, Sally Martineau, and Pat Williams.

Nancy and Dennis Rogers who tried to teach me cross-country skiing.

A dream team of encouraging friends—Mimi Villhaume, Florence McCarthy, Linda and Carol Heen, Charlie Boone, Peggy Singh, Joan Sorenson, The Kenwood Ladies, The St. Charlies, and more. Many more. My thanks are true and endless.